This Isle is Full of Monsters: Shakespeare's Audiences and the Supernatural

By Jon Kaneko-James

Published by

Greenock, Scotland

www.beulaithrispublishing.co.uk

Copyright 2018 © Jon Kaneko-James

First Edition

ISBN: 978-0-9957784-1-2

Acknowledgements

The author would like to acknowledge all the fantastic people without whom this book would not exist: Michael and Mandy at Beul Aithris, David Saunderson of The Spooky Isles, Andy Mercer, David Waldron and Paula McBride, Tracey and Mark Norman, all of his colleagues at Shakespeare's Globe, Keroko James for not divorcing him, not to mention the staff at various libraries and archives over the years, particularly those at The Keep in Brighton.

He would also like to dedicate the work to his brother, Dr Michael David James, and to the game of Dungeons & Dragons, without whom the path of study that led to this book might never have been embarked upon.

Contents

A Supernatural World

William Shakespeare was christened on April 26th 1564 and died on April 23rd 1616. His life saw a huge number of changes – from Elizabeth's vulnerable early queenship to becoming the mythologised Gloriana: a fairy queen and figure of worship. He saw theatre companies rise from travelling players to become entrenched and wealthy staples of the royal court. He saw the early stewardship of King James I and the rise of the English language (being one of a generation who were registered born in Latin and dead in English).

More than that, Shakespeare lived at the beginning of the last era where the state regularly and routinely endorsed the existence of the supernatural. While researchers have shown a popular belief in witchcraft (in the historical sense, rather than the Neopagan or Wiccan religious movements) continuing into the 19th century, Shakespeare's lifetime was the last period of English history where the machinery of government itself endorsed belief in the supernatural.

Some of these figures can be seen in Shakespeare's plays, and will be the subject of this book: witches, magicians and fairies. Others would have been the meat and drink of everyday life. The fifth book of Foxe's *Acts and Monuments* devotes an entire section to supernatural retribution handed out to those who partook in the persecution of Protestants during the Marion persecution. Here, we see the fate of the greedy Sheriff Woodruff who burned Protestant John Bradford:

"…not long after [he] was stricken by the sodayne hande of God, he lyeth yet to this daye benumbed and bedred in his bed, not able to move himself."[1]

On the same page as Foxe's tale of Sheriff Woodruff, he tells us the tale of Doctor Leyson, sheriff at the burning of Bishop Farrar, who helped himself to the dead man's cattle:

"…doctor Leyson… had afterward fet awaye þe said byshops cattel, from his seruantes house, called Mathew Harbottel, into his own custody said the cattel coming into the Sherifes custody, diuers of them would neuer eate meate, but lay bellowing and roaring, and so died."[2]

The rising tide of Providentialism taught citizens to believe that a supernatural force was guiding their lives and punishing them for their ills. Children were getting possessed by the Devil in towns from London to Lancashire. Foxe described the 1588 storm that stymied the Spanish Armada as a direct intervention by God:

"Flavit et dissipati sunt" ("He [God] blew and they were scattered").

And there certainly were those who, within the bounds of the 16th and 17th century mind-set, did not believe in the supernatural. Reginald Scott's hugely influential 1584 book *The Discoverie of Witchcraft* not only set out a stall of scepticism against the witch trials, but against other areas of the supernatural as well:

"But certeinlie, some one knave in a white sheete hath cousened and abused manie thousands that waie; specialie when Robin good-fellow kept such a coile in the countrie. But you shall understand, that these bugs speciallie are speid and feared of sick folke, children. Women and cowards, which through weakness of mind and bodie, are shaken with vaine dreames and continuall feare… in our childhood our mothers maids have so terrified us with an ouglie divell having hornes on his head, fier in his mouth, and a taile in his breech, fanges like a dog, clawes like a beare… and a voice roring like a lion, whereby we start and are afraid when we heare one crie bough: and they have so fraid us with bull beggers, spirits, witches, urchens, elves, hags, fairies, satyrs, pans, faunes, sylens, kit with the cansticke, tritons, centaurs, dwarfes, giants, imps, calcars, conjurors, nymohes, changlinges, Incubus, Robin good-fellowe, the spoorne, the mare, the man in the oke, the hek waine, the fier drake, the puckle, Tom thombe, hob gobblin, Tom tumbler, boneless, and such other bugs, that we are afraid of our owne shadowes…"[3]

Even Richard Bancroft, who would one day become the Bishop of London (and eventually Archbishop of Canterbury) preached against spirits with the same fervour that he worked against Puritans and the idea of demonic possession. In a 1589 sermon in St. Paul's churchyard he said:

"Believe not in everie spirit… but trie these spirits whether they be of God…"

For the citizen, though, these were enchanted times: housewives saved their pennies to buy talismans from magicians and Cunning Men like Arthur Gauntlet and Simon Forman. A housemaid at a townhouse just off the Strand knelt in the marshy grass for hours in the hopes of meeting the Queen of the Fairies. Witches upon witches went to the gallows, with Londoners in 1603 able to read about the bloody witch hunt perpetrated by their new king.

It would be a mistake to think that these people were less intelligent than us, or less able to discern reality from fantasy. The calculations that a London craftsman would be able to accomplish in his head, or with a few marks in the dirt, would put many modern practitioners to shame. Certainly, the average English grammar school boy would possess a knowledge and fluency in Latin that would put many 21st century classicists and historians to shame.

And so, as these citizens – with their lives full of witches, sorcerers and fairies – stood in the yard of the Globe to watch *Macbeth*, or sat crowded on the benches to watch *A Midsummer Night's Dream*, or even went across the road to the Rose to enjoy an afternoon with *Doctor Faustus*, what was the substance of this supernatural world around them? What would they have expected in reality? Finally, how were the lives of these liminal people themselves?

Selected References

[1] John Foxe, *The Unabridged Acts and Monuments online or TAMO*, 1563 edition, HRI Online Publications, Sheffield, 2011, Book 5, p. 1785. www.johnfoxe.org [accessed 03/09/17]

[2] Ibid.

[3] Reginald Scott, *The Discoverie of Witchcraft*, 1584 edition, EP Publishing, 1973, p. 122

The Magicians

At riper yers to Wittenberg he went,
Whereas his kinsmen chiefly brought him up.
So much he profits in divinity,
The fruitful plot of scholarism grac'd,
That shortly he was grac'd with a doctor's name,
Excelling all, and sweetly can dispute
In th'heavenly matters of theology;
Till, swollen with cunning of a self-conceit,
His waxen wings did mount above his reach,
And, melting, heavens conspir'd his overthrow;
For, falling to a devilish exercise,
And glutted now with learning's golden gifts,
He surfeits upon cursed necromancy;
Nothing so sweet as magic is to him,
Which he prefers before his chiefest bliss…
-- Prologue, The Tragical History of the Life and Death
of Doctor Faustus, Christopher Marlowe, (1591)

On August 20th 1507, a Benedictine abbot called Johannes Trithemius wrote about a man named Georg Sibellicus the Younger, who was calling himself Georg Faust: "Faust, who dared to call himself the Prince of Necromancers, is a vagrant, a charlatan and a rascal."[1] According to Trithemius, Faust had been travelling around Germany making wild claims. In Gelnhausen he had claimed a complete knowledge of Plato and Aristotle, in Wurtzburg he said that he could replicate Christ's miracles on demand, and in Kreuznacht he said that he was the most learned alchemist who had ever lived.

The humanist Konrad Muth wrote about how a Georg Faustus had been bragging at an inn that he had untold prowess at fortune telling. Tales of Faustus-like activities even came up during Martin Luther's table talks: just as Marlowe portrays Faustus as putting horns on the head of a knight who has vexed him, Luther tells a story of the Emperor Frederick inviting an unnamed necromancer to dinner who first turns a guest's hands into claws, and then adds horns to the Emperor's head. Likewise, one popular folktale of Faust being able to eat improbable amounts of matter is mirrored in a Luther story of a man who is taken for a monk eating a cartful of hay.[2]

Despite this poor reputation, Faust's self-promotion made him a magnet for myth. He died in 1538 and even by then there were stories about him. The chronicler Wolf Wambach collected tales of the Erfurt area in 1550, and there were already scores of local anecdotes about him. It was Wambach's chronicle, written with Kilian Reichman and now lost, that was amongst the first to call Faustus 'Doctor', and that amplified the diabolical connection between Faustus and his magic.

The popularity of Faust probably came about due to the equal popularity of the Teufelsbucher, or 'Devil's Books', which were stories of the ordinary men's encounters with the Devil. These stories ranged from horror, to fantasy and comedy. All were staunchly moralistic and showed the need for good Christian faith in the face of the Devil's temptations. It's a similar tradition to the stories expressed in sermon books popular in Britain at the same time, citing the stories of Caesarius of Heisterbach, John of Salisbury and Walter Map, who wove lurid fantasies with moral messages.

The first glimmer of the iconic woodcut we see in early editions of Marlowe's *Faustus*, appears in a Teufelsbuch called *Die Zauber Teufel* from 1553.[3] Similar to the picture of Faustus we see in the woodcut of a sorcerer in a circle conjuring – although there seem to be enough of these to suggest that they were a genre in their own right – we see a Medieval illumination of the pilgrim from Lydgate's *Pilgrimage of the Life of Man* meeting a student of necromancy standing in a magical circle.[4]

It was fairly natural that in the country that had invented printing, Faustus was going to get a book of his own. In 1587 Johannes Spiess published the first Faustbook. It was little more than a narrative version of all the various folktales about Faust already in circulation at the time: Wolf Wambach had already written about how he had made the apparitions of Hector, Achilles and Priam appear before his students in Wittenburg, and how he'd gotten a scare when the giant Polyphemus had refused to depart. The same chronicle, which a later writer called Zacharias Holler used, also said that Faustus confessed to a Franciscan friar that he'd sold his soul to the Devil.

This Faustbook borrowed heavily from the writings of sceptics and humanists who were seeking to dampen, rather than fuel, the witch persecutions. Reginald Scott's *The Discoverie of Witchcraft*, JohanWier's *De Praestigiis Daemonum*, or, '*Tricks of the Demons'* and Augustine Lerchiemer's *Christian Memory and Witchcraft* all donated stories to the Faust corpus.[5] In this collection, Faustus deprives a priest of his Breviary (a book of liturgical rites); Faustus eats a hake he had not cooked (stealing food by magic was a big theme of German sorcerer stories, and even some witch trials); Faustus shaves a priest's beard. There are strange ones, like where Faust causes his guests to almost cut their own noses off by making them hallucinate succulent grapes. Oh, and the one where Faustus eats a young man whole, drinks a glass of water, and then the young man is found alive – soaking wet and shivering in a closet – a while later.

By 1588 Faustus had been through a re-edit at the hands of two university students from Tubungen, who had reduced the number of stories and eliminated some of the duplications. It's this edition that came to the UK sometime between 1590 and 1592 (it was printed in 1592, but both Elizabeth Butler and Professor Owen Davies argue that there was probably a bootleg handwritten translation available in manuscript as early as 1590).

It's this book, called *The History of the Damnable Life and Deserved Death of Doctor John Faustus*, that Marlowe seems to have used for his Faustus. It was translated by a mysterious figure called 'PF Gent', probably signifying he was a gentleman. Some say this was John Dee – a mathematician, cleric and magician who communicated with angels – which Owen Davies finds unlikely since there are plenty of existent samples of John Dee's writing, and it has none of the playfulness, lightness or sense of humour present in PF's work.
PF cuts down on the torture porn, emphasises Faustus' courage and curiosity, and builds up the fantastical, mystical imaginings of the Faust story. He also goes a critical step towards humanising Mephistopheles by cutting out scenes where Mephistopheles mocks Faustus, and by having him refuse to humiliate and intimidate an

old man who first tells Faustus to turn his back on the Devil and mend his ways.

What Marlowe's play brings to the table is verisimilitude. He cut a lot of stories to fit into the runtime, eliminated duplication, and then added a few subtle but interesting details. It's from Marlowe's *Faustus* that we get the real details of conjuration: the circle; incantations; sharing books with fellow conjurers and the whole strata of less well-educated conjurers like Wagner, and the two stable boys Robin and Dick.

One of the big sources for Marlowe's *Faustus* might well have been the same books that Spiess plundered: Reginald Scott's *The Discoverie of Witches*, and Johan Wier's *Tricks of the Witches*. Both had an attention to detail that completely defeated their initial intentions. They contained such detailed accounts of practical magic that both books were often sold as books of magic in and of themselves. In fact, one section of JohanWier's book, the *Pseudomonarchia Demonum* is now well-known as a directory of demonic entities in its own right.

It's also possible that Marlowe knew either one or both of a pair of Cambridge demonologists (a name for clerics or devout Christians studying demons and sorcery) named Robert and Henry Holland. Both were around Cambridge roughly the same time as Marlowe, with Robert studying for his master's at the same time as Marlowe was pursuing his BA.[6] Henry even wrote a book about witches dedicated to Robert Devereux, someone who we know was in Marlowe's literary orbit.[7]

In 1590, when Marlowe was writing *Faustus* and the PF Faustbook was in circulation, Henry Holland was the Vicar of St. Brides. Marlowe and the Holland brothers would have been able to get their hands on plenty of magical books while they were in university at Cambridge. As we shall hear in *The Merry Devil of*

Edmonton, universities were considered sources of magical books.

Another major aspect of the magic that gave birth to Faustus' summoning was the adaptation of Jewish Kabbalah into the growing corpus of Natural Magic. This was the work of Ficino's student, Giovanni Pico della Mirandola, a young nobleman and all-round genius who spoke at least four languages by the age of 23. He received a number of Kabbalistic texts from his language tutor, which he translated from Spanish into Latin and used to fuse Hebrew mysticism with Hermetic practice. While Ficino's practice had been passive – using natural forces to heal, bring money or good luck – Pico's new method was aggressively humanistic: now, instead of passively accepting the divine, sorcerers could bring angels themselves down from heaven to dispute, teach and act for them. In Pico's system humans can even communicate directly with God, at the risk of a phenomenon known as 'the death of the kiss', or dying from an overload of supernatural ecstasy.

Once they have this, why can they not communicate directly with something else? And rather than a voluntary merging with angels, why can't they achieve a more selfish mastery over demons?

Soon all this is tied together and popularised in the work of Heinrich Cornelius Agrippa Von Nettesheim. Agrippa was an adventurer and soldier whose biography presents us with a real-life counterpart to Marlowe's Faust. Georg Faust had the name, but Agrippa led the life; his output crossed every field of endeavour: theology, magic, law, philosophy… he was even an early writer in gender studies, writing a book called *In Praise of Women*. He was an adventurer and soldier who, while working as a mercenary, crossed into Italy and came into contact with the works of people like Pico and Ficino, spurring him on to take a couple of months out of his busy schedule and revolutionise the world of Natural Magic as well. However, Agrippa: he was never dragged to hell… but he was never a demonic sorcerer either. He wrote his *Three Books of Occult Philosophy* in 1510, with them seeing publication in 1533, which was ironically after he had disavowed magic and decided it was all bunk, tearing all magical theories to pieces in his 1526 book *De Vanitate*. This is the real Doctor Faustus: a man who passes through magic on the way to even more radical thinking.

The Magician Prospero

ARIEL: All hail, great master! Grave sir, Hail! I come
To answer thy best pleasure; be't to fly,
To swim, to dive into the fire, to ride
On the curl'd clouds, to thy strong bidding task
Ariel and all his quality.
PROSPERO: Hast thou, spirit,
Perform'd to point the tempest I bade thee?
ARIEL: To every article.
I boarded the king's ship; now on the beak,
Now in the waist, the deck, in every cabin,
I flamed amazement. Sometime I'd divide,
and burn in many places; on the topmast,
The yards and bowsprit would I flame distinctly,
Then meet and join. Jove's lightnings, the precursors
O' the dreadful thunder-claps, more momentary
And sight-outrunning were not; the fire and cracks
Of sulphrous roaring the most mighty Neptune
Seem to besiege and make his bold waves tremble,
Yea, his dread trident shake.
-- Act 1, Scene 2, The Tempest, William Shakespeare,
(1611)

The image of a magician like Prospero would have been familiar to the audiences of early 17th century London. As a fairly late play, it came in the wake of works such as *The Wisdom of Doctor Dodypoll*, featuring an upstart middle class doctor, which would have appeared on the stage around a decade earlier; productions of the legendary *Doctor Faustus* abounded both in London venues and as far afield as Exeter. The popular early play *Sir Clyomon and Sir Clamydes* contained the noble magician Sir Bryan Sans Foy, who keeps a garden of earthly marvels and provides a fantastical rite of passage for the two noble knights. In the noted piece of

Shakespeare apocrypha, *The Birth of Merlin*, again, the character of Merlin is a semi-antagonist: he provides a fantastical rite of passage for Uther Pendragon and later reels off exposition on the future of the nation of the Britons.

In the classic Shakespearean fashion, Prospero's magic is a 'black box'. He presses a button and Ariel advances the plot, unlike the more naturalistic portrayal of Faustus' magic from Marlowe, or the satires on magic penned by Jonson. Another viewpoint, though, could be that Prospero is a post-ritual magician. Marlowe's Faustus is in the process of striving at the beginning of the play, like Jonson's less successful Fitzdotterel, but Prospero has finished with the rings, swords and circles of ritual magic. Ariel and the other spirits are bound. The work is done.

Another complication for the island-dwelling Prospero – and a reason to cast him as a sorcerer whose spirits are already bound – is that a magician would need quite a number of ritual magical tools. The latest edition of Folger manuscript V.b. 26 – a magician's collection of spells from the 1580s – compiles a list of the various accoutrements needed:

Amulets
The Book (consecrated as is detailed in V.b. 26 itself)
A circle (drawn in the soil with a metal instrument, or sometimes with chalk, oil, or palm ashes)
Fire, sometimes made with special wood such as elder or thorn
Food offerings for the spirits
Fumigations or incense, as well as various noxious substances to punish uncooperative spirits
Garments, as in de Abano's *Heptameron*, a priestly garment, or a garment made of white linen
Ink

Oil (usually olive)
Parchment
A pen and pen stand
Pentacles of kidskin parchment
A ring inscribed with the name 'Tetragramaton' for controlling spirits. Another ring as described in V.b. 26 for enclosing a spirit
Rose water
A sceptre
A scryer, usually a virgin child
Scrying stone, crystal ball or 'glass'
Sword
Table
Hazel wand
Water
Whistle[8]

Every item would not just need to be owned, but specially made, stored and consecrated. The owner of Cambridge University Library *MS Additional 3544*, writing in the mid-16th century, records methods that show what would be involved for a magician to prepare his magical tools:

"Of the needle and another instrument of iron, how etc.

Many indeed are the experiments which are done with a needle, concerning which it is written that an iron needle or stylus should be made; on a Thursday and in the hour of Jupiter; and it should not be finished on that day or in that hour, but bring it to completion on Friday and in the hour of Venus…"[9]

Making a wand is a little easier:

"Of wands and Rods and other instruments.

If rods or wands are needed, it does not matter which woods the wands are made of; and cut it with one blow with a knife at the root in the hour of Mercury. And let the same characters be written on the wand with the aforementioned colouring, which are written in the experiment of preparation of the iron instruments, as of the knives, etc."[10]

Each of these guides from *Additional 3544* proceeds from instructions of preparation into a magical oration that will bring the final consecrated power upon the item. The book also contains similar rules regarding swords, although not Prospero's signature staff. Both the pentacle and ring would be needed to act as armour against the possibility of spiritual attack.

Once bound, theoretically, a spirit would come when called and be relatively obedient to the magician, if it came at all. Certainly the real books of magical spells collected by magicians in the 16th and 17th centuries contain fewer spells to control an uppity spirit that has been bound, than they do to make spirits appear, obey, and arrive without harming anyone.

The act of getting the spirit in the first place, however, was more fraught. V.b. 26 contains extensive instructions for summoning various spirits. From the start of the book, the magician has to complete a series of 'pre-flight' checks. Not only must the magician have prayed extensively for his own soul, but next he must pray for his assistants, for the purity of the water used to bless things, for the fire used to light candles and burn incense, and over his extensive array of ritual items.

Once the full series of prayers had been said, the real work of the magician would begin: conjurations were long and repetitive, with formulas of God names, magical words, threats and poetic images. Magicians would cross themselves innumerable times as indicated by the text. Many times, we can infer that the spirits would either come slowly, or not come at all.

In V.b. 26, directly after the owner has recorded instructions on how to summon a spirit into a consecrated looking glass or stone, they have written a conjuration with the following, most telling, header:

"Then after the consecration of your book and stone what spirit soever… you may call with this Call if he come not at the first, call till he come and doubtless but he will come."
Afterwards, we have another heading that gives us little cause for optimism: "Say as followeth three times if he come not at the first, and then straight ways he will come."
Then another: "If he comes not, say as followeth…"[11]

When the spirit finally comes, things might not initially be very pleasant:

"With these things duly completed, boundless visions will appear, and phantasms beating on devices and all sorts of musical instruments, and it is done by the spirits in order to terrify the associates and force them to flee from the circle, because they are able to face the master himself. After this you will see boundless archers with the boundless multitude of awful beasts, which compose themselves thus, as if they wish to devour the associates. However, they have nothing to fear. Then the priest or master, holding out his hand to the pentacle, should say: 'Fugiat hinc Iniquitas bestra virtute vixilli dei.'

And then the spirits will assemble to obey the master, and the associates will see nothing further."[12]

Once a spirit was successfully called and dealt with once, it would be licensed to depart with an injunction to return. We see this in the relationship between Prospero and Ariel, who certainly doesn't require Prospero to draw up a circle or perform an elaborate ritual, and certainly comes when called. The fairly verbose V.b. 26 has a comparatively brief license to depart:

"I conjure thee, spirit or spirits, and that now by the virtue of our Lord Jesus Christ, the which was put upon the cross for you and all you spirits, that you and every one of you do return into your proper places, and by the virtue of the high God, and that you do nor hurt me, nor yet none other creature, but that now forthwith you do return unto your proper places, and that when I shall call you, or any of you, to answer unto me again or to give me that I shall require or desire, and that you do it quickly and that with all obedience, to be ready to come and fulfil my request and commandment, rede, rede, rede in pace, and the peace of Jesus Christ be now between you and me and that in the name of the Father + and the + Son + and of the Holy Ghost. Amen. Three persons in Trinity and one God in Unity be rendered all laud, praise, and dominion, both now and forever, world without end. Amen."[13]

For Faustus, the story is his progression from pact to perdition and the struggle for his soul along the way. We follow Faustus from before his conjuring of Mephistopheles to his eventual end, and during the section of the play which I call the 'Adventures', Faustus is seen to achieve wonders of entirely a like kind with Prospero. The former Duke of Milan lacks Faustus' playfulness, as we see in the way he uses his spirits to chase Caliban, Trinculo and Stephano, and the way he sends Ariel as a harpy to reprimand the 'three men of sin' for betraying him. If Prospero had any discernible sense of humour, his status during *The Tempest* and *Doctor Faustus*' during third act could be almost identical.

A key difference, however, is a characterisation of Prospero's spirits that marks him not as a duke of Milan, but instead very much as the product of a British writer using British influences. With the possible exception of Caliban – who seems like something between a nature spirit and what the English would have called a 'prodigious' birth – there is no evidence that Prospero's spirits are in any way demonic.

We see a variety of spirits in a number of other manuscripts. V.b. 26, the manuscript that to my mind is closest to the sort of book that Prospero may have been able to bring with him after his exile from Milan, has a number of different categories of spirits. Close to the beginning of the book there is a 'Prayer for one's Angel' – for the communication and protection of a guardian angel not unlike the partly psychic good angel who tries to protect Faustus – along with an experiment on how to use seven angels on different days of the week to attune your magic. There are spells for demons such as the horned and hooved Baron – whose name, under another spelling, is mentioned during the trial of Joan of Arc – and for the fairly neutral seeming planetary spirits.

Other spells stray into the realm of fairy: V.b. 26 contains two spells for 'Oberion', and a set of seals for 'Mycob', the Queen of the Fairies. Similarly, in the Medieval book *eMus 137* held at the Bodleian Library, we find a set of directions calling a spirit into a crystal: not a demon, but Oberon, called and bound using the names of God and terrible words of power. The same manuscript also contains the spell *Experimentum Optimum Verissimum for the Fairies*, a folk technique for courting the good graces of fairies by leaving a bucket of water in a place where they are known to appear, and then skimming off the rime to enhance the attractiveness of a series of offerings.

The manuscript *Ashmole 1406* gives us a lengthy conjuration for a fairy called Elaby. Like the conjuration in *eMus 137*, it is structured in the same way as other Medieval conjuration: the sorcerer prepares a circle and then drags Elaby into a prepared location by invoking various angels, archangels and names of God. *1406* even gives us a spell that Prospero could very well have used to summon and bind the spirit Ariel:

"An Excellent way to get a Fayrie… First get a broad square christall or Venus glasse in length and breadth 3 inches, then lay that glasse or christall in the bloud of a white henne 3 Wednesdays or 3 Fridays: then take it out and wash it with holy aqua and fumigate it: then take 3 hazel sticks or wands of an yeare growth, pill them fayre and white, and make soe long as you write the spirits name, or fayries name, which you call 3 times, on every sticke being made flatt one side, then bury them under some hill whereas you suppose fayries haunt, the Wednesday before you call her, and the Friday following take them uppe and call hir at 8 or 3 but when you call be in cleane Life and turn thy face towards the east when you have her bind her to that stone or Glasse."[14]

In fact, Prospero's most obvious displays of magic have a good deal in common with the fairy magician as depicted in *The Wisdom of Doctor Dodypoll*. After sending Ariel as a harpy to threaten those who deposed him as Duke of Milan, Prospero creates a spiritual banquet for the lovers Miranda and Ferdinand, something that audiences would have seen in *Dodypoll* a decade earlier: as the lovers Lassingbergh and Lucilia wander in the forest they encounter a troupe of fairies under the control of a wandering conjurer who berates them (the fairies) for thoughtlessly giving a jewelled cup to a passing peasant, before abducting the lovers and using his magic to try and get his way with the beautiful Lucilia. (He fails, because love is stronger than magic).

As the Enchanter rebukes the fairies we see some language that reminds us strikingly of both Ariel and Caliban:

ENCHANTER: Where is my precious cup you Antique flames,
Tis thou that hast convaide it from my bowre,.
And I will binde thee in some hellish cave,
Till thou recover it againe for me.
You that are bodyes made of lightest ayre...
--The Widsom of Doctor Dodypoll, Act 3, Scene 3

The Enchanter, with his troupe of spirits, was a staple of both Medieval and Early Modern mythology regarding sorcerers. After the polymath Heinrich Cornelius Agrippa died in 1535, possibly contributing his biography to the character Doctor Faustus, his two black dogs – Monsieur and Mamselle – were mythologised in a single demonic hound that acted as his familiar.

The anatomy of the stories found in plays such as *The Tempest*, *Dodypoll* and *Faustus* is a mixture: equal parts Medieval chronicle, folktale and wild rumour. However, while there were men – as we see in the case of Georg Faust – who laid claim to feats not unlike those of Prospero and Faustus, few, if any, of them were noblemen.

Selected References

[1] Karl P Wentersdorf, "Some Observations on the Historical Faust", *Folklore*, Vol. 89, No. 2, 1978, p. 201

[2] William Hazlitt (ed), *The Table Talk of Martin Luther*, Bell & Daldy, 1872, p. 251

[3] Owen Davies, *Grimoires: A History of Magical Books*, Paperback Edition, OUP, 2010, p. 50

[4] This is described in the text: John Lydgate & F J Furnival (ed), *The Pilgrimage of the Life of Man*, The Roxburgh Club, 1905, p. 496; the image itself is London, British Library, MS Cotton Tiberius VII, fol. 47; a version of it can be seen in Richard Keickhefer, *Magic in the Middle Ages*, Canto, 2000, p. 172

[5] Elizabeth M Butler, *The Fortunes of Faust*, Magic in History Series, Sutton, 1998, p. 7

[6] Leonard W Cowie, "Holland, Robert (1557–1622)", *Oxford Dictionary of National Biography*, Ed. H. C. G. Matthew and Brian Harrison. Oxford: OUP, 2004. Online Edition. Ed. David Cannadine. Sept. 2010. 6 Sept. 2017 http://www.oxforddnb.com.ezproxy2.londonlibrary.co.uk/view/article/13540

[7] Henry Holland, *A Treatise against Witchcraft; Or, a Dialogue, Wherein the Greatest Doubts concerning That Sinne, Are Briefly Answered. ... Hereunto Is Also Added a Short Discourse, Containing the Most Certen Meanes Ordained of God, to Discover, E[x]pell, and to Confound All the Sathanicall Inventions of Witchcraft and Sorcerie*, Cambridge: J. Legatt, 1590

[8] Daniel Harms, James R Clark and Joseph H Peterson, *The Book of Oberon: A Sourcebook of Elizabethan Magic*, Llewellyn Publications, 2015, pp. 18–19

[9] Francis Young (tr.), *The Cambridge Book of Magic: a Tudor Necromancer's Manual*, Texts in Early Modern Magic, 2015, p. 110

[10] Young, p. 117

[11] Harms, Clark and Peterson, pp. 95–101

[12] Harms, Clark and Peterson, pp. 52–53

[13] Harms, Clark and Peterson, p. 314

[14] K M Briggs, "Some Seventeenth-Century Books of Magic", *Folklore,* Vol. 64, No. 4, Dec 1953, p. 458

Nobles and Magicians

The typical relationship between a conjurer and nobleman can be found in a letter written by the early 16th century magician William Stapleton.

Stapleton had been a monk at St. Benett's in Norfolk, but had found the life difficult. Just before leaving the Order he had been forced to seek a dispensation to avoid Matins due to not being able to rise in time, and had been given a period of time away from the Order to raise the money to buy himself out of his life as a cleric.

From his own letter, he also seems to have found the most basic duties of a monk too burdensome, stating not only, "I had often been punished for not rising to mattins…" but also, "…and [not] doing my duty in the church."

During this time, it would seem that Stapleton started on the road to becoming a conjurer. He threw in with one John Keever to purchase two magical books and the equipment for invoking spirits: the books *Thesaurus Spirituum* and *Secreta Secretorum*; and conjuring equipment such as a magical ring, a specially inscribed plate, a circle and a 'sword for digging'. These items he claimed to have kept for six months, adding two more books to his collection – texts on using magical invocation to find buried treasure that completed a collection of magical paraphernalia that their contact had supposedly bought from the Vicar of Wotton.

William did not find buried treasure, but his magical skills were sufficient to peak the interest of one Richard Thony, who paid 46s 8d to help buy him out of his life as a monk; perhaps even funding the subsequent trip to London, where Stapleton bought a hermit's licence, which he took back to his circle in Norfolk,

where he was once more asked to use his magic
to procure money.

While this might seem a world away
from the high magic of Prospero, purportedly
being able to use magic to find treasure led
Stapleton to a new life of hobnobbing with the
upper set. After procuring a magical book
(supposedly once owned by the Parson of
Lessingham) into which the spirit 'Andrew
Malchus' had been bound, he bought a Cunning
Man's summoning equipment and started a
summoning group with the knight Sir John
Leiston, failing because Malchus was allegedly
already working for Cardinal Wolsey.

After an attempt to bind the spirit
'Oberion' with the help of magical seals kept
(supposedly) by Sir Thomas More, Stapleton
seems to have caught the eye of a glazier named
Tynney and been taken to Walsingham to work
for a man whom Stapleton refers to as 'Lord
Leonard Marquess', who supposedly lived at
'Calkett Hail', probably Caldicott Hall, outside
Fritton.

During this time Stapleton seems to
have also attempted to scry for another noble
magician, Sir John Slepe, along with his ritual
partner, Sir Robert Porter – both probably
clerics – at 'Creke Abbey', although there is no
mention of whether they were able to find
treasure.

Whether or not his endeavours with Sir
John and Sir Robert went well, Lord Leonard
seems to have been intent on getting the most
out of Stapleton, and the pressure looks to have
put him to flight. Leonard challenged Stapleton
and a man named Jackson to use their magic to

find treasure that he himself had hidden in his garden – a test Stapleton's letter suggests they failed.

Surprisingly, Lord Leonard was not put off. He took Stapleton in as a secular priest, and a while later the Hall's cook persuaded Stapleton and Sir John Leiston to seek treasure on Bell Hill. This seems to have been the breaking point for Stapleton. After a completely unsuccessful attempt at finding the treasures believed to lie in the earth around Bell Hill, Stapleton took his equipment and fled to London, where Lord Leonard had him committed to prison for leaving his service without permission.

Finally – whether by intrigue or entrapment – Stapleton left prison and spent a while working for the Parson of Wornstowe, Sir John Ratcliff, from where he attracted the eye of a man named Wright, in the pay of the Duke of Norfolk.
Perhaps having heard of his remarks that Cardinal Wolsey had summoned the spirit Andrew Malchus, Norfolk's servants urge Stapleton to intervene against a spirit sent to torment him by the Lord Legate, Cardinal Wolsey.[1]

Obviously, as a man attempting to avoid death by execution, at this point Stapleton's narrative concentrates on his absolute innocence, although the fact remains that he has worked, by this point, for a number of noblemen – albeit clerics – a possible marquis, and a duke.

Another ill-fated attempt at magic that shows the relationship between magician and nobleman involves the 1544 case of Lord Henry Neville, son of Ralph, Earl of Westmorland. A family retainer – and con man – Ninian Menville seems to have manipulated Lord Henry's gambling debts to the point where he was prepared to allow Menville to introduce him to the magician 'Wisdom', named like a character in a Ben

Jonson play, who purported to be able to create a magical ring that would allow him to triumph in games of chance.

Wisdom claimed to be a doctor by trade, who only performed magic for his dearest friends, and offered to make the ring in return for a lifetime pension of £20 a year. This would have been a huge sum of money for Lord Henry, who seems not to have had the wherewithal of Lord Leonard. Lord Henry seemed to believe Wisdom's claim that the ring would make him £2000–3000 in the few weeks before Christmas.

Wisdom told Henry that the ring could be made to contain either a good spirit or evil, although both would work "by the holy angels" and that it would be of nothing but virtue, convincing Lord Henry sufficiently that he only bargained Wisdom down to £10 a year, but allowed the sorcerer to move into the Neville household.

What followed was undoubtedly a confidence trick, but also came directly from the textbooks of Renaissance magic: Wisdom spent over a month coming and going at the Neville house, explaining to the perturbed Lord Henry that he was only able to work on the ring between the hours of 3–4am and 5–6pm because "[the angels] must be taken, before their matins and after their evensong."

The idea of favourable astrological hours was a staple of the idea of 'natural' magic, and books of spirit conjuration. Such ideas were present in the 14th to 15th century *Sworn Book of Honorius*, and other contemporary magical texts like the various

Books of Solomon. By the 18th century, in some editions of the *Grimorum Verum* – a popular book of spirit invocation, if not ring making – there were often headache-inducing spirals known as 'The Circle of the Hours' which provided a complete table of the hours so that magicians would always know when to work with a certain planet during the days of the week.

Lord Henry's dabbling with magic would first lead him to a hastily abandoned magical spectacle in his own drawing room: after giving Wisdom £4 to purchase expensive magical paraphernalia (including bolts of expensive cloth), a slab of wax for an altar and four candles, he had to abandon his summoning of 'The God Orpheus' when a neighbour knocked on the door and the host missed the magical hour while hastily entertaining him.[2]

Such ceremonies were characteristic of the nobles' fascination with magic: Gilles de Rais, French nobleman and comrade of Joan of Arc, employed a number of magicians. One anonymous magician worked alone in a separate room to the Lord de Rais. His accomplice – a man named Gilles de Sille – bade de Rais remain in a magical circle, where he reported that he could hear the conjurer in the next room being beaten mercilessly by the demons he had summoned.

When a ceremony went well, the effects it could create were images reminiscent of the fantastic horrors that Shakespeare had portrayed as inhabiting Prospero's island. In the diaries of the Italian adventurer Benvenuto Cellini, he describes striking up a friendship with a Sicilian priest who offered to engage a necromancer friend to show Benvenuto a host of demons.

The summoning took place at night in the Colosseum, where the priest drew elaborate circles and burned malodorous perfumes that drew legions of demons who filled the amphitheatre. They demanded another session with a virgin present before they would grant Benvenuto's wish of being brought together with the girl Angelica.

Whether the second part ever happened is a matter for interpretation. Benvenuto's story borrows heavily from Caesarius of Heisterbach's *Dialogues Miraculorum* and one of the *Comedies of Horace*: Benvenuto brings one of his shop boys, a good friend named Vincenzio Romoli, and his friend Agnolo Gaddi.

When the necromancer made an even more elaborate circle and burned yet more perfumes to the spirits, this time they used the servant boy as a medium for speaking with the spirits. If the story is to be believed, Benvenuto held the young man under the pentacle while the necromancer invoked in Hebrew, Latin and Greek.

This time things went wrong: although the demons promised that Angelica should come to Benvenuto within the month, the demons were out of control. The boy cried that there were "a million tremendously fierce-looking men there… [and] four enormous giants…", causing the companions to fear for their lives. Benvenuto tried to cheer the companions on, but the panicking child cried that there were flames rushing towards them.

While Benvenuto ordered Gaddi to throw some asafoetida at the demons, the Horacian element came into play:

"The instant he went to make a move, Agnolo blew off and shat himself so hard that it was more effective than the asafoetida. The tremendous stench and noise made

the boy lift his head a little, and when he heard me
laughing he plucked up courage and said the demons
were running away like mad. We stayed where we were
until matins were rung. Then the boy spoke up again and
said that there were only a few devils left, some distance
away from us…"[3]

The Magicians – Upstart Crows

To entertain the subject of our play,
Lend us your patience.
'Tis Peter Favell, a renowned scholar,
Whose fame hath still been hitherto forgot
By all the writers of this latter age –
In Middlesex his birth and abode,
Not full seven mile from this great famous city –
That, for his fame in sleights and magic won,
Was called the merry fiend of Edmonton.
Of any here doubt such a name,
In Edmonton, yet fresh unto this day,
Fiz'd in the wall of that old ancient Church,
His monument remaineth to be seen,
His memory yet in the mouths of men,
That whilst he liv'd he could deceive the devil…
-- Prologue, The Merry Devil of Edmonton, Anon.,
(1608)

There would seem to be a number of blueprints for a magician: the first was a commoner, often of high intelligence, who was either well-educated or self-educated, and had inducted himself into either the professional trade of conjuring, or an allied trade like medicine. The second, a cleric or former cleric, either petty nobility or from the ranks of the middle classes, fallen into magic for want of a better living.

The self-educated magician finds fellows in Marlowe's Wagner, Robin and Dick. Growing literacy and a greater availability of texts meant that by the time Marlowe was alive, the educated weren't the only people practising magic. Dominican Inquisitor Johannes Nider talks about a bard called Benedict who practised magic, had a frighteningly monstrous appearance and led a violent, dissolute life. Nider's writings show us that unlike Faustus he was able to put aside his magic, eventually finding a monastery which took him in after his sister's prayers softened his heart, although the former sorcerer was haunted by demons for the rest of his life.

In the French village of Nancy, in 1593, a resident called Nöel le Bragard was arrested for magic. He was said to have been a magical healer who, like Agrippa, started off as a soldier. He told a story of how one of the town gatekeepers had a magical book that allowed him to find lost things and provoke love, which Bragard was jealous of. Bragard knew a soldier who had a similar book, but wouldn't loan it to him, and eventually got his own magical books after he found an old woman with a collection of magical papers that she kept locked up in a chest. Bragard said that he bought the whole lot, transcribed them, and sold them on.

In Nancy, Bragard was arrested, his books were taken, and he was eventually executed after a long period of torture[4] but for most magicians, death would have been the least likely outcome. Owen Davies of the University of Hertfordshire analysed the existing records for European witch trials and found that only 4% of all witch trials focused on defendants who modern researchers would recognise as really having practised magic.[5] Heinrich Cornelius Agrippa, writer of the *Three Books of Occult Philosophy* and influential on western magicians for generations, was despised by some but allowed to live until he died of natural causes, having turned away from magic as his life went on.

Therefore, it isn't that hard to imagine Faustus practising magic, moving from one court to another, even being specifically invited to places by various nobles and rulers because of his magical skill: both John Dee and Cornelius Agrippa did exactly that, with John

Dee being invited to Bohemia by Vilem, Lord Rosenburg, and Agrippa to Cologne by the Archbishop-Elector respectively. Both were eventually too hot for the areas they'd been invited to (and the leaders who invited them) to handle, but both managed to find a new place and continue their practices.

Another well-known commoner magician was the London physician Simon Forman, alive and active during Shakespeare's lifetime, and even mentioned in Jonson's *The Devil is an Ass*.

From the Salisbury area, he had garnered a little schooling in Wilton, at a free school run by a shoemaker turned cleric named William Rydout, learning to read and write with a certain amount of difficulty and quite a few beatings. Afterwards he did well enough to be sent to the grammar school at the Close of Salisbury Cathedral, where he was technically a boarder, although the reality of it seems to have involved being a house elf for a miserly canon called Mintern, who kept him warm by making him carry logs up and down through the house.

Unfortunately for Forman, when his father died, his mother decided an extra pair of hands to work the farm was more important than a son with education, and so he was brought back to tend the family farm until he successfully apprenticed himself to a shopkeeper and chancer named Matthew Commin. He almost instantly reneged on his promise to let Forman return to the grammar school in Salisbury, despite having bound his apprentice for ten years instead of the usual seven.

Despite this, Forman learned how to make medicines, and built up his education by assisting a wool merchant's son who attended the Salisbury Grammar and boarded with the Commins. It was sufficient to allow Forman to break off his apprenticeship (since his master had failed in his obligations by not really teaching him anything, and not allowing him to attend grammar school) and briefly return to grammar school, before taking a teaching post at the Wilton free school where he himself had been educated.

It was around this point that Forman took his first steps into magic by buying a book on the works of Galen, the 2nd century physician upon whom the core of Early Modern medicine was based. This, and Forman's education in the liberal arts, would have first taught Forman astrology, which was thoroughly interwoven with the medicine of the time.

Simon Forman's casebooks are filled with astrological charts, which, next to uroscopy – the literal study of urine – was one of the only methods of diagnosis left to Early Modern doctors if the cause of a patient's illness did not readily present itself.

Forman himself wrote, "…astrologie is the booke and course of all naturalle things, the grounds of physicke and mother of all artes what so ever. And without that thou canste doe nothing in physicke nor magick."

We even see Forman's use of magic directly in his treatment of patients. Forman used the techniques found in Early Modern magical books to cure illnesses. The manuscript *Harley 273* in the British Library contains a spell to cure fistulas, boils and wounds which involves a thin sheet of lead with five crosses inscribed on top, while reciting five Our Fathers. The magician would then make three holes in the sheet, speaking three more Our Fathers and the charm, "I conjure you,

[unfilled name], to heal the fistula, boil or
wound in the name of the five wounds suffered
by Our Lord Jesus Christ, in the name of the
Holy Trinity and the three nails that crucified
Our Lord Jesus Christ, in the name of the Holy
Passion, without risk or suffering."[6]

We can see the action of something
similar in Forman's work, from this story by the
astrologer William Lilly, whose mistress owned
a magical seal created by Forman to cure her
husband who was afflicted by a spirit that
tempted him to cut his own throat. In this, we
see the use of magical seals:

"She many times heard him pronounce 'defie thee' and
she desired him to acquaint her with the Cause of his
Distemper, which he then did. Away she went to Dr.
Simon Forman, who having framed his sigil and hanged
it around his neck, he was wearing it continually until he
died and was never more molested by the spirit: I sold it
for 32 shillings."[7]

Forman's notebook contains detailed descriptions of
magical seals used for magical protection from illness,
which he sold for a pretty penny.

Forman, however, also engaged in
summoning magic and divination. He wrote in
his diary in 1579, "This yere I did profecie the
truth of many things which afterwards cam to
passe, and the very sprites wer subjecte unto
me, what I spake was done."

Over the next few years Forman's
diary sometimes describes his making the same
kind of specialised invocation tools that
William Stapleton describes, culminating in a
series of magical experiments with the scryer

John Goodridge. One Halloween in 1597, Forman recorded in his diary:

"The said spirit apeare and said that he walked ther for killing of his father. And he caste out moch fier and kepe a wonderfull a doe but we could not bringe him to humain form, but he was seen like a great black dog & trobled the folk of the house moch & fered them." Likewise, just after All Hallows Eve in November, Forman wrote, "This night he cam according to his wont & raued moch & we bound him strongly, & kept him till almost 4 of the clok in the morning..."

We can surmise, however, that Forman's efforts weren't satisfactory, because he also cast an astrological chart to know, "whether ever I shall haue that powr [power?] in nigromantic that I desire or bring it to effect."[8]

The Magicians – The Clerics

The fact that some clerics were conjurers can be proven
beyond question. Even without the, admittedly, slightly
suspect testimony of Benvenuto Cellini and the
surprisingly frank letter/confession of William Stapleton,
we read a description of a scholarly cleric/magician in
the works of John of Salisbury:

> "During my boyhood I was placed under
> the direction of a priest, to teach me psalms.
> As he practiced the art of crystal gazing, it
> chanced that he after preliminary magical
> rites made use of me and a boy somewhat
> older, as we sat at his feet, for his
> sacrilegious art, in order that what he was
> seeking by means of fingernails moistened
> with some sort of sacred oil or chrism, or of
> the smooth polished surface of a basin,
> might be made manifest to him by
> information imparted by us.
> And so after pronouncing names which by
> the horror they inspired seemed to me, child
> though I was, to belong to demons, and
> after administering oaths of which, at God's
> instance, I know nothing, my companion
> asserted that he saw certain misty figures,
> but dimly, while I was so blind to all this
> that nothing appeared to me except the nails
> or basin and the other objects I had seen
> there before."

> -- John of Salisbury, *Policraticus Book I, p.
> 165*

The exact origins of the Universities are obscure. The term 'universitas' simply meant a group of people, or a corporation, at the start of the Medieval era. Over time the term began to be applied to Universitas Scholarium and Universitas Magistrorum – corporations of students, and corporations of teachers.

The rise of the universities as independent bodies of learning arose from the need to teach subjects that extended beyond the ecclesiastical curriculum. Cathedral schools like Paris, York and Chartres mastered and dominated learning. Not only were other subjects needed, but bodies of learning arose from regions that had dominated a particular topic: Bologna got its own Universitas Scholarium after already excelling in matters of law, while the Salerno, the first Western university, was purely a medical school.

Even at slightly less religious Universitas Magistrorum, or guilds of teachers, with chancellors instead of rectors, the structure of the Medieval university was fairly monastic: students entered at fourteen so long as their Latin was fluent enough, studied grammar, logic, and the Latin version of Aristotle's treatise on rhetoric. Once they had finished this course, known as the Trivium, they moved onto the Quadrivium: a course on arithmetic, geometry, music and astronomy. Once they had done this they could enter a Master of Arts degree and teach themselves. If they wished a doctorate, qualifying them in theology, canon law, civil law or medicine, a further eight years' study was required.

We see how suitable this education was to those wishing to study magic in the birth of the whole system of 'natural' magic, using the passive influences of astrological forces upon objects and images. In 1460 a Byzantine monk bought a copy of *The Corpus*

Hermeticum to Florence, where it was translated by the priest, doctor and thinker Marsillio Ficino.

Ficino then produced a body of Neoplatonic Theories, which argued that everything was interconnected. The signs of the zodiac and the astrologically active planets permeated everything: every plant, animal and stone. Colours, words, shapes and even music could connect man to God by the power of astrology. He argued that this was a purely natural form of magic, inbuilt into the universe, which became part of a school of thought known as Natural Magic.

There were certainly magical books abounding at universities. The 13th century Bishop of Paris, William of Auvergne, gave a catalogue of magical books that he'd seen while attending the University of Paris:

The Major Circulus
The Minor Circulus
De Deo Deorum
The Annuli Saturni
The Rings of Solomon
The Sign of Solomon
The Nine Scarabs
The Entoca
The Liber Sacratus
The Mandal
The Almadel

William even described using mystical, if not magical, visionary practices:

"I even thought that gradually by abstinence and by abstracting my soul from the solicitudes and delights that held it captive and submerged it in the inferior world, which is the sensible world, those things that were obscuring and clouding my soul might be broken by contrary habits, and the chains and bonds extinguished, and thus my free soul might evade them, and be able to break forth free and capable through its very self into the superior region, which is of the light."
-- William of Auvergne, *De Universo*[9]

After William's time, in 1398, the University of Paris went so far as to release a document condemning various magical practices, including a vivid description of students invoking a spirit:
"...the great circle conscribed with divers unknown names and marked with various characters, the little wooden wheel raised on four wooden feet and a stake in the midst of the same great circle and the bottle placed upon the said wheel, above which bottle on a little paper scroll were written certaine names, whose meaning is unknown to us, forsooth Garsepin, Oroth, Carmesine, Visoc, with the sign of the cross and certain characters interposed between the said names, and also thrones, earthen pots, a fire kindled, suffumigations, lights, swords and many other characters and figures and divers names and known words and also the naming or writing of the four kings on four nall paper wheels, forsooth, King Galtinus of the North, King Baltinus of the East, king Saltinus of the south, King Ultinus of the west, with certain characters written in red interposed between the names of the said kings; considering also the time and the suspect place and the behaviour of those who were present.... The things they did after oaths had been taken by them many times as to the making of a legal division of the treasures to be found...

[and] in a certain room in which were the said instruments, superstitious in themselves, with lights lit and suffumigations about the bottle and circles, in which were the said inscriptions and the said characters, and the said co-workers, stripped to the waist in their smallclothes, holding swords by their hilts each one before a throne, sometimes fixing the points in the earth and sometimes circling about with the said swords near the thrones and circles and bottle, raising the points of the swords to the sky, and sometimes placing their hands together with the hand of the protagonist over the bottle, which he called holy and in which… should come the spirit…"[10]

Another factor, certainly in Pre-Reformation England and the Catholic Europe where Prospero would have operated, was the ordination of students into nominal clerical roles. Some students would have taken their tonsure in order to secure further education, while others may well have intended a career as a priest but decided to do something else with their lives.

At such an early stage, they would have been sworn into a minor, largely defunct, role such as wrangler, door-keeper, lector… or exorcist.

With the newly tonsured student clutching his book of exorcisms, Prospero's Europe had seen the birth of a new type of magic, fusing the Hebraic magic text with Neoplatonism and Catholic ritual in a quest for personal gain.

This magic incorporated a wide variety of spirit summoning, magical items and utility spells (such as spells to become invisible, to inspire love or to catch a thief). The techniques of that magic, as we have seen reproduced in the University of Paris text, kept their wording very close to that of the traditional exorcism. Rather than glorying in the forces of darkness and hailing Satan, the necromancer was a holy operative, constraining demons and spirits with the names of God.

Consider here a traditional exorcism:
"I adjure you, ancient serpent, by the judge of the living and the dead, by your Creator, by the Creator of the whole universe, by Him who has the power to consign you to hell, to depart forthwith in fear, along with your savage minions, from this servant of God... Therefore, I adjure you, profligate dragon, in the name of the spotless + Lamb, who has trodden down the asp and the basilisk, and overcome the lion and the dragon, to depart from this man (woman) + (on the brow), to depart from the Church of God + (signing the bystanders). Tremble and flee, as we call on the name of the Lord, before whom the denizens of hell cower, to whom the heavenly Virtues and Powers and Dominions are subject, whom the Cherubim and Seraphim praise with unending cries as they sing: Holy, holy, holy, Lord God of Sabaoth. The Word made flesh + commands you; the Virgin's Son + commands you; Jesus + of Nazareth commands you, who once, when you despised His disciples, forced you to flee in shameful defeat from a man; and when He had cast you out you did not even dare, except by His leave, to enter into a herd of swine. And now as I adjure you in His + name, begone from this man (woman) who is His creature. It is futile to resist His + will. It is hard for you to kick against the + goad. The longer you delay,

the heavier your punishment shall be; for it
is not men you are contemning, but rather
Him who rules the living and the dead,
who is coming to judge both the living and
the dead and the world by fire."[11]

Contrast this with a spirit conjuration from the *Munich Book*, a 15th century manuscript of spells found in the Bavarian State Library and properly named '*CLM 849*'. The book was the working spellbook of a magician, probably a cleric, and the clerical roots of the conjuration can clearly be seen:

"I command you, O most wicked dragon, by
the power of The Lord and adjure you in the
name of the lamb without blemish who
walks on the asp and the basilisk, and who
had trampled the lion and the dragon; you
may carry out quickly whatever I command.
Tremble and fear when the name of god is
invoked, the god whom hell fears and to
whom the virtues of heaven, the powers,
dominions and other virtues are subject and
to whom they fear and adore, and whom
cherubim and seraphim praise with untiring
voices. The Word made flesh commands
you. He who was born of a virgin
commands you. Jesus of Nazareth, who
created you, commands you, to fulfil at once
whatever task that I ask of you, or all that I
wish to know. For the longer you delay in
doing what I order, the more your
punishment will increase day by day. I
exorcise you, O accursed and lying spirit, by
the words of truth."[12]

And so, for a real-life Prospero, it was much more likely that rather than performing the magic himself, he would have a cleric or hermit, on hand to perform works of magic for him. If a kept cleric was not to his taste, he might have invested in a magically operative businessman like Simon Forman or the shady necromancer Wisdom.

Selected References

[1] A very readable account of this can be found for free on archive.org in: Percy Millican, *Norfolk Archaeology: or Miscellaneous Tracts Relating to Antiquities of the County of Norfolk*, 1847, pp. 57–64

[2] An excellent summary of this is in: Alec Ryrie, *The Sorcerer's Tale*, Electronic Edition, OUP, 2010, pp. 18–51

[3] George Bull and Benvenuto Cellini, *The Autobiography of Benvenuto Cellini*, Revised Edition, Penguin, 1998, p. 197

[4] Davies, 2010, p. 64; also, Lorraine Archives (Nancy Office), B 7309/1, witch 120, Nicolas Noel dit le Bragard, 1593, via http://witchcraft.history.ox.ac.uk/pdf/w120.pdf

[5] Owen Davies, *Popular Magic: Cunning-folk in English History*, Hambledon Continuum, 2003, p. 9

[6] British Library Digitised Manuscripts, Harley MS 273, ff 70r–85v, accessed via: http://www.bl.uk/manuscripts/FullDisplay.aspx?ref=Harley_MS_273

[7] Barbara Howard Traister, *The Notorious Astrological Physician of London*, Works and Days of Simon Forman, University of Chicago Press, 2001, p. 97

[8] Traister, pp. 105–107

[9] Thomas Benjamin de Mayo, *The Demonology of William of Auvergne*, Thesis, University of Arizona, pp. 47–52

[10] Alan Charles Kors and Edward Peters, 'The University of Paris Condemns Sorcery' translated and transcribed in *Witchcraft in Europe 400-1700: A Documentary History*, Revised Edition, University of Pennsylvania Press, 2001, pp. 129–130

[11] One good example can be seen in Rev. Basil Stegmann, *Prayers to Expel Evil Spirits*, Pamphlet, Joseph F Busch, 1945, pp. 17–18

[12] "Impero tibi, draco nequissime,per imperium dominicum. Adiuro te in nomini agni inmaculati, qui ambulat super aspidem et basciliscum, qui conculcauit leonem et draconem, ut fcias cito quidquid precipiam. Contremisce et time, invocato nominee dei, quem inferi timent, quem celorum virtutes et potestates, dominaciones et cirtutes, et alie subiecte sunt et timent et adorant, quem cherubin et seraphin indefessis vocibus laudant. Imperat tibi natus ex virgine. Imperat tibi Iesus Nazarenus, qui te creavit, ut cito impleas omnia que a te petam vel habere voluero vel scire desidero. Quia quanto tardius feceris que tibi precipio vel precipiam, tibi supplicium magis crescit et crescat de die in diem." Richard Kieckhefer, *Forbidden Rites: A Necromancer's Manual of the Fifteenth Century*, Sutton, 1997, p. 280

Magicians, the Devil and Temptation

Ay, they do now name Bretnor, as before
They talk'd of Gresham, and of doctor Forman,
Franklin, and Siske, and Savory (he was in too);
But there's not one of these that ever could
Yet shew a man the devil in true fort.
They have their crystals, I do know, and rings,
And virgin Parchment, and their dead men's sculls,
Their raven's wings, their lights, and pentacles,
With characters; I ha' seen all these.
-- Act 1, Scene 2, The Devil is an Ass, Ben Jonson,
(1616)

Here we see Jonson's gullible would-be magician
Fitzdotterel mention his magical influences – including
our friend Simon Forman. The idea of a wealthy man
being sucked dry by charlatans trying to summon spirits
would have been a familiar story to Jonson's audience.
While Forman charged highly for his services – he once
charged a promiscuous countess 29s and 6d for a coral
ring that would enhance her sex appeal,[1] with a promise
of £5 extra if it worked – there's no evidence he was a
confidence trickster, unlike the magicians Gresham and
Savoy, of whom we'll hear more.

It was a different matter in the case of Gilles de
Rais, the general who fought alongside Joan of Arc.
While Gilles was said to have committed terrible war
crimes while fighting in 15th century France, he was
certainly not so fearsome a figure that he was immune to
con artists.

When the French nobleman's fortune waned
due to his unwise spending he had, in desperation, turned
to necromancy and demonology in the effort to raise it
higher. Unwilling or unable to perform the spells himself
he employed a procession of magicians to try and either

find buried treasure for him or summon demons who could give him riches. Some were unsuccessful and admitted as much, while others – like one pair of operators who injured themselves while in the circle to try and convince de Rais that their demon had attacked them. Most of these men had simply taken de Rais' money and given him wonderful acts of theatre – lavish rituals and impressive conjurations – but had not supplied much beyond apologies and some luridly narrated visions via magical mirrors or crystals.

Even the famous magician John Dee was assisted by the much less reputable Edward Kelly. Kelly was an aspiring alchemist and necromancer who struck up a partnership with Dee while visiting his house in the hopes of using one of his necromantic books. Even now historians cannot decide whether their partnership was equal, or whether Kelly was playing Dee for a fool. Certainly it ended by being more trouble than it was worth, because Kelly was eventually forced to flee the country with Dee when his political enemies turned against him.

The Sight of Spirits

The one feature that marks both Faustus and Prospero out as puissant magicians, exempt from the heaps of scorn that Jonson pours on the various aspiring magicians in his own works, is that both men are able to perceive the spirits they command – whether angelic, demonic or fairy – unaided. We see the same thing in *The Merry Devil of Edmonton*, where our magician is able to see and command his demon without resort to any assistant.

However, Londoners' expectations of the magicians living around the 16th and 17th centuries would be far different. As we have already seen from the narrations of John of Salisbury and Benvenuto Cellini, magicians did not expect to see with their own eyes what they were summoning. Instead, they worked with various visionaries, or 'scryers': the magician John Dee had Kelly, Simon Forman had Goodridge, the lesser-known Goodwin Wharton had his lover and eventual wife, Mary Parish.

These scryers had a great deal of power over the magicians they worked with: there was the constant unease and mistrust between Dee and Kelly, with Dee more than once referring to Kelly as a 'cosener'; Mary Parish's ever closer relationship with Goodwin Wharton as she promised him power and status in the fairy kingdom. The perceived deficiency of magicians unable to see for themselves is something that we see in diaries and magical books again and again.

In Simon Forman's diary for 1594, he wrote on August 23rd, "I dremt I did see in a glas when I did call and that I did heare alsoe, & and that yt was the first tim that euer I did heare or see I was aunswered directly of all thinges."[2]

Returning to Jonson's *The Devil is an Ass*, Fitzdotterel's opening monologue – delivered as Fitzdotterel himself attempts to conjure the Devil – gives us a possible opening into how a magician might have felt at his perceived spiritual blindness:

Would I might see the devil. I would give
A hundred o' these pictures to see him
Once out of picture. May I prove a cuckold
(And that's the one main mortal thing I fear)
If I begin not now to think, the painters
Have only made him. 'Slight, he would be seen
One time or other else. He would not let
An ancient gentleman, of as good house
As most are not in England, the Fitz-dottrels,
Run wild, and call upon him thus in vain,
As I ha' done this twelvemonth.
-- Act 1, Scene 2, The Devil is an Ass, Ben Jonson,
(1616)

Magicians being magicians, their books are filled with spells to grant them the same sight as their scryers. In Sloane MS 3851, *The Grimoire of Arthur Gauntlet*, a 17th century magician who employed local woman Sarah Skelhorn to scry and see spirits for him, he nevertheless inscribed 'A Prayer whereby to have sight of the Angels'; a ritual 'To call three good Angels into a Crystal Stone or looking Glas to theine own sight…'; and a spell 'to call the Angels into a Glass of Water' which specifies: "…I charge you and command you and bring you that you come into this Glass & bring all that do belong unto you for to show me anything that I shall ask or desire that I may plainly behold it with my mortal Eyes."[3]

Similarly, the various owners of V.b. 26 also filled their book with methods to see the spirits. Towards the middle of the book, one of the owners records two recipes for an ointment and tincture that would permit the seeing of spirits:

"Take the herb fleabane, sicorda, garmene, and the tree that swimmeth which is said arbor cancri, and malie with rore madii, and with the tree that showeth at night called herba lucens, and with these make an ointment and put thereto the eyes of a whelp and the fat of a hart, and anoint thyself and it will make open the air unto thee, that thou mayest see spirits in the clouds of the heavens, and all so there by thou mayest go surely, whither thou wilt, in one hour."

And also, "Take the herb giant fennel, which is dreadful and grievous and very strong in operation. Take the juice of it, the juice of a cicute, or water hemlock, henbane, tapsibar-bati, red sandalwood, and black poppy. With this confection made, thou mayest fume what thou wilt, and thou shalt see devil and strange things, and if apium were joined therewith. Know that, from each place suffumed, devils should fly, etc."[4]

V.b. 26 contains a number of variations on the theme involving the blood of a lapwing to make an ointment, complete with a fantastical backstory for the recipe involving an invisible Turk. There is also an extremely prolonged spell that involves killing a white howlet, a lapwing, a black hen, a black cat, a mole, a bat, and a raven. This involves fermenting them in a magical vessel, and using them in a ritual to summon a beautiful spirit who will anoint the magician's eyes in order to allow him to see spirits almost whenever he desires.

This spell is formidable, and shows to some degree the desperation of the magician to see this impermeable spirit world for himself. If the owner of V.b. 26 ever attempted the spell, it would have taken weeks: several days for each animal, whose blood had to be kept in a specially prepared and sealed vessel until a specific astrological day and hour before the next step. Each animal required a spell, and the whole affair involved appealing to powers as diverse as 'Inferiors and servants to the Empress and princes of all fairies…', King Solomon, Prince Arthur, 'Sibbells' and a variety of otherwise lesser-known spirits whose names appear only in this spell.

Certainly, a little examination can reveal why a magician might want to take the job of scrying out of the hands of someone as unreliable as a scryer: anyone reading the account from John of Salisbury can readily imagine the difficulties of using children, if a child can even be persuaded to go along with the spell. In a trial of 1607 at the town of Rye the magician Anna Taylor tried to replace her demanding and unreliable scryer – also her tenant and neighbour – Susanna with one of her own children. Unfortunately, at least according to Susanna, the experiment failed. On both occasions where the child was taken to give an offering to the fairies, he just cried until Susanna took him back down to his mother's parlour.[5]

The famous partnership of John Dee and Edward Kelly was more volatile still. Kelly came to Dee's house on false pretences, disguised as a Catholic named Talbot, and even once his identity was reconciled he continually argued with those around him, swinging between declaring his visions to be angelic, demonic, and false. Even the relationship between the nobleman Goodwin Wharton and his visionary Mary Parish – which resulted in their marriage – was fraught with deceptions, half-truths and continual arguments.

Neither Prospero nor Faustus seem the sort to tarry with such things, although both have a secondary magician: for Faustus it is his servant Wagner, the subject of a book of his own in the Germanic Faustus tradition. For Prospero, we can see a little of the resentment and antagonism between Dee and Kelly in his relationship with the vile and fishlike Caliban, albeit transposed into the monster's disclosing to Prospero the various secrets of the isle:

[I] show'd thee all the qualities o'th'isle,
The fresh Springs, brine-pits, barren place and
Fertile.
Cursed be I that did so!
-- Act 1, Scene 2, The Tempest, William Shakespeare,
(1611)

The Magical Life

...that a brother should
Be so perfidious! –he whom next thyself
Of all the world I loved and to him put
The manage of my state; as at that time
Through all the signatories it was the first
And Prospero being the prime duke, being so reputed
In dignity, and for the liberal arts
Without a parallel; those being all my study,
The government I cast upon my brother
And to my state grew stranger, being transported
And rapt in secret studies.
-- Act 1, Scene 2, The Tempest, William Shakespeare,
(1611)

It would be reasonable to expect an educated man such as Prospero to have a fair education in Latin. That a fair number of Early Modern noblemen were literate in Latin is hardly a controversial claim. It is even possible that the young Prospero had attended university, simply without receiving his BA/MA. He could well have come into contact with works of magic such as the sort that William of Auvergne listed, or that perhaps, like John of Salisbury, he might have been a part of the works of a chantry cleric whose downtime involved invoking spirits for magical treasure.

However, while the life of a magician able to summon and bind spirits like Ariel and the goblin-hounds that chased away his three insurrectionists might be easily attainable for a man living alone on a haunted island, it would be fairly debilitating to a man tasked with running the city of Milan.

One influential book on the life a magician should lead as they approach a magical operation is Peter de Abano's *Heptameron*. We can see its influence by its relative ubiquity when it comes to magicians' workbooks: elements from the *Heptameron* can be found in V.b. 26 and in Sloane MS 3851 – *The Grimoire of Arthur Gauntlet*. The earlier MS Additional 3544 (hailing from somewhere between the late third and early fifth decades of the 16th century) doesn't contain any *Heptameron* material, but contains material from books that informed the *Heptameron*, such as the more directly Jewish influenced *Liber Ratziel*.

The *Heptameron*'s comment on purity begins to show us the strictures that would be on both Faustus and Solomon: "The operator ought to be clean and purified by the space of nine daies before the beginning of the work, and to be confessed, and receive Communion… The master therefore ought to be purified with fasting, chastity, and abstinency from all luxury for the space of three whole dayes before the day of the operation. And on the day that he would do the work, being clothed with pure white garments…"[6]

We see a similar influence from Semitic ritual magic, and of the requirement of ascetic purity, in V.b. 26. After several injunctions to purity and fasting, the author elaborates upon the purity a magician must achieve before suffumigating his chamber for magic: "Note they that suffumigate observe or ought to do seven things, for so Solomon said the hermits did, and attained to their desire.

1. They used abstinence or fasted.
2. They washed and cleansed themselves.
3. They did alms.
4. They slew and cast blood into the fire.
5. They pray much in hours, i.e. times in the day and times in the night.

6. They made fumigation with good things and
    well smelling as above, and they attained to
    their petitions, by the commandment of the
    creator.
7. They slew and burned all."

In another section, the compiler of V.b. 26 goes into
more detail:

"The master that worketh must purify himself by seven
days before the work. He must wash himself; he must eat
nothing of theft, neither of raven, neither of evil party,
neither any thing unclean, neither that is fallen to death,
neither of any beast of four feet, nor of none other, and
he must eschew from evil malice and falsehood. He must
not drink wine nor eat fishes nor anything with blood
goeth fro. He must not join to a woman to pollute
himself, nor menstruate, nor enter into a house where is a
dead man, nor go to the grave of a dead man, nor by him
that suffereth and the law hath condemned. Avoid pride,
be clean, continue in prayer, keep thy tongue from
slandering, lying, and swearing, fast truly, keep thy bed
warily, and avoid sin. Light thy house with prayer, praise
ye angels, do alms, remember the needy, and forget not
the works of mercy and be joined not to evil men. Clothe
thyself with clean clothes, trust in god, be faithful, have a
good hope, and use appellation in all necessities to the
creator…"[7]

The book also contains extensive instructions on the
magician's procedure for ritual washing. These are no
easy baths to be run by a palace servant:

"You must go to a running fountain or a flowing stream,
have warm water ready for a bath. Then remove all your
clothes, and say these psalms: 'The Lord is my Light';

'The fool has said'; 'I said: I will take heed'; 'Save me O Lord'; 'Let us sing'; 'Give Glory'; 'Whoever will be saved.'

"And when you are naked as you were born, enter the bath or water, and the exorcist should say:
"[Latin prayer]

"And when you have been washed, emerge from the bath, making the sign of the cross and saying, 'In the name of the Father' and you should sprinkle exorcized water on your face, saying, 'thou shalt purge me with hyssop, O Lord,' etc. Then, put on your clothes while saying these Psalms: 'O Lord, rebuke me not'; 'Blessed are they'; 'Hear my prayer, O Lord'; 'Out of the depths'; 'When I called upon him'; 'I will give praise'; 'O how I love'; 'When Israel went out'; 'When the Lord brought back'; 'O lord you have tested me'; and this following oration:
"[Lengthy Latin prayer]"[8]

MS 3851, *The Grimoire of Arthur Gauntlet*, believed by David Rankine to originate from the early decades of the 17th century, contains similar injunctions and procedures. In fact, while much of Gauntlet's magic followed the same expectation of usually seven days of ritual preparation (sometimes extended to nine, or abbreviated to three), later in his manual he describes an even more lengthy period of observance if he should like to call upon good spirits:

"Whosoever therefore would call upon a good Spirit that he might have sight and conference with him must observe two things especially, Of the which the one is about the disposition of the caller, The other concerning those things which are put to the prayer outwardly for

the conformity of calling the Spirit. Therefore it
behoveth the caller himself now to be religiously
disposed throughout many days unto such a mystery.
First he ought to be contrite and confessed inwardly and
outwardly and rightly to satisfy God, every day washing
himself in holy water. Futhermore that the caller doth
keep himself through these whole days, Chaste,
abstinent, with a mind altogether untroubled and that he
separate himself from all external and secular business
whatsoever as much as he can. Also he must observe
fastings these days according as it shall seem to him to
be able to perform, And daily also Let him make his
prayers from the East Sun, even to the west to God and
the Angels to be called on, in the place of his invocation
being clothed with a holy and linen vestment. Seven
times let him do it without interruption or being let in his
business. But the number of days of preparation is
commonly a whole Month of the Moon: but another
number observed with the Cabalists is forty days."[9]

This shows the roots of Gauntlet's spell in another book,
the *Liber Juratus*. This book, again a merging of Semitic
magic with Byzantine and Latin Christianity, contains
either a 40 or 72 day core ritual (depending on the
edition of the book – the 'London' *Honorius* contains the
longer ritual, while others do not) followed by 20 days of
ritual purification along the lines that we have seen
already.
        Finally, to perform the spell the
visionary must construct a special sleeping
environment:

"On Thursday begin in the morning; saying as you said
on the preceding, and then you should make a bed of
hay, on top of ashes which you should make clean from

the dregs, and around the bed, in the ashes, should be written the one hundred names of God…

"Then he should put on a sackcloth and black garments and enter the [bed], in which he should sit. Then he should begin the Psalter with the litany, and with the proper prayers and the rest as mentioned before, and when all is complete, he should say these names as follows…

"Then he should sleep, speaking to no one, and thus it will happen that he will see the heavenly palace, and the grateness of his glory, the orders of angels and multitudes of blessed spirits…"

He then wears a hair shirt and special garments, ritually washes himself in spring water, and performs a long invocation, after which he will recline and see a vision of God.

What's more, since an excerpt of V.b. 26 has already made reference to a specially consecrated book, what would be the logistical realities of such a consecration? According to the *Liber Consecrationum*, or *The Book of Consecrations*, the magician's book would only hold its magical efficacy by a familiarly punishing process of ritual activity. The magician should refrain from any type of pollution of the mind or body, fast for nine days before his spell, keep from idle or immoderate words, and always be clothed in clean garments. During these nine days, he must attend mass with the magical book under his arm and place it on the altar during mass. Once the book is charged, he must place the book in a hidden place, sprinkled with holy water and wrapped in a priestly stole.

Other books go further: some require no contact with women for days on end. Considering the stipulation in V.b. 26 that women's sexuality and menstruation are both impure, it can be inferred that an operator engaging in a ritual from the *Liber Juratus* would need to avoid women for weeks on end. Or perhaps set his servants to quiz women on their sexual appetites and the state of their menstruation, which would do little for his reputation, even in 16th century Europe. Most spells require prayers at specific parts of the day, sometimes at the dead of night, and frequent confession.

All imply secrecy, withdrawal from the world and a set of obligations that are far from social. For a man trying to run a city, this could prove, at best, complicated. Further, some of the spells might require Prospero to physically leave the city of Milan. In British Library Sloane MS 3824, a prototype of a better-known magical book called the *Lemegaton*, the author describes the sort of space that a magician would require in order to invoke spirits:

"To call forth Pemersiel or any of these his Servants, choose the uppermost private or secret and most tacit Room in the house, or in some certain Island, Wood or Grove, or the most occult or hidden place from all comers and goers that no one chancily may (if possible) happen that way…"

Granted, like Faustus, Prospero might well be able to seek an empty chamber at the top of his ducal residence in order to seek communication with spirits, but the mention of an island is interesting: was his ending up there with Miranda an accident? In this chapter we have already seen how much infrastructure Prospero might have needed in order to pull off the sort of magical tricks he plays on the Milanese invaders. Could it be that after ousting him from his seat, poetic justice saw him stranded on the very island where he had sought to work his magic?

In V.b. 26, in a section on working with magic circles that wears its links to books like the *Lemegaton*, and other works of Solomonic magic, on its sleeve, the magician describes a very similar set of requirements for a space to invoke spirits:

"This house or chamber must be in a void place, and not near the course of men, for the opinion of some expert men in this art, is that spirits are more willing to appear in some waste place, as in woods, heaths, fens, moors, downs, or in any place where is no great resort, nor where none of the seven sacraments have been ministered, for they hold opinion the place is holy where such is practised. Be warned."

Even the comparatively down to earth Arthur Gauntlet records a very telling aphorism in his magical book:

"Aphorism: 3:

Live to thy Self and thy learning. Avoid the friendship of a multitude. Be covetous of time."

At worst, as Duke of Milan, Prospero would have been a vague absentee – unable to engage in the socialisation required of his station, unable often to wear the clothes of his rank. To the modern reader this may sound enticing, but the practicalities of such a man might well not have left Prospero in any condition to be an effective leader – nine days without food or drink will hardly leave a man well prepared to orchestrate trade deals or judge disputes between courtiers. Being constrained to avoid worldly troubles might look, to the casual onlooker, like weakness or laziness. Vanishing for seven days to conduct a spell would hardly be conducive to the business of state.

Thus we see a new dimension to the end of Prospero the magician: not only breaking his staff and drowning his book to turn his back on magic – which, by this point has been conclusively useful and only ever profitable for him – but in order to be an effective Duke of Milan. By setting Ariel free and leaving the island, he puts his body and soul in the worldly realm where his people live. Working not for a thoroughly personal and selfish form of enlightenment, but finally to benefit his family and his city.

Selected References

[1] Anne Somerset, *Unnatural Murder: Poison at the Court of James I*, Orion Publishing, 1997, p. 79

[2] Traister, p. 107

[3] David Rankine (ed), *The Grimoire of Arthur Gauntlet: A 17th Century London Cunning-Man's Book of Charms, Conjurations and Prayers*, Avalonia, 2011, p. 105, 113 & 138

[4] Harms, Clark and Peterson, p. 158, 159 & 358

[5] TNA RYE 1/13/8

[6] Peter de Abano and Joseph H Peterson (ed) (tr), *Heptameron: Or Magical Elements*, Digital Edition, 2008, presented as a web page without pagination:
http://www.esotericarchives.com/solomon/heptamer.htm

[7] Both this and the above spell are on Harms, Clark and Peterson, p. 161

[8] Harms, Clark and Peterson, pp. 483–486

[9] Rankine, pp. 200–201

Demonic Possession

The number of artworks depicting the Devil, demons or creatures related to them is almost uncountable for the 17th century alone. From the woodcut artwork of pamphlets on witchcraft – like the devil depicted in the 1591 work, *News From Scotland* – to the strutting, cocksure devil in Thomas Potts' 1612 book on the Pendle witches, or from the crude devil depicted in the English edition of the *Faustbook*, to a strange newsletter about a devil who made crop circles in Hertfordshire, it is clear the Devil was an everyday part of Early Modern life.

At some point in the early 17th century, a matter-of-fact business letter between John Allin and Phillip Frith of Sussex records an appearance of the Devil at a mayoral election in the village of Rye. Allin writes of the King of France's trouble with Parliament and where England might send its troops in the Low Countries. He then blithely mentions that the Devil appeared during the business of the town corporation, played the fiddle, vanished for a moment, then reappeared to strip a man, take some of his hair and his flesh, and leave him in a state near death. The letter then almost seamlessly goes back to discussing the shipping and trade out of Portsmouth.[1]

For Ben Jonson's audience, the Devil was also hidden in place names, and in the very association with theatre. Anti-theatre preachers referred to playhouses as "The Devil's Pulpit" and "Temples of Satan", while they might have been familiar with The Devil's Neckinger, a site of punishment near the Neckinger River, now underground. They might have drunk at The Devil's Tavern in Wapping, now the Prospect of Whitby, had business riding through Devilden Woods in Croyden, or visited the equally satanically named Scratchwood in Barnet.

In Early Modern drama, plays were chock full of devils, or mentions of them. Quite aside from the still-famous devil in Faustus, devils – and devil-shows where characters faked the appearance of the Devil – were common in the Early Modern love of spectacle. Audiences might have been treated to *The Bugbears* – a farce where a group of young men convince a rich man that his house is haunted in order to steal money – or *The Puritan*, where a con man pretends to summon a devil by magic in order to gull a wealthy widow out of her fortune. They might have sat and watched Hecate in *The Witch*, where we don't see the Devil himself, but a catalogue of his works, from a witch with a lifespan far beyond the human norm. While certainly not all Londoners in 1616 believed in the Devil as a physical presence, he was certainly a part of their daily life.[2]

Temptation and Demonic Possession

For some Early Modern Londoners, Satan was an ever-present force behind wicked deeds and bad thoughts. We have only to see the records of the possession of the Middle Temple lawyer Robert Brigges from 1574 to see the role of the Devil as the force behind intrusive, unpleasant thoughts. Both of the records of Brigges' possession include the passage, "...desirous to adresse and dispose himselfe to devotion in the meydest of his prayers, the devil wolde thrust into his troubled mynde sume tymes desperate suggestions that he had sined against the holy gost, that he was a reprobate and therefore prayed in vayne, sumtym uncleane thoughts, sumtyme blasphemius imaginations against the magistey of God."[3]

Protestant Reformers had been keen to avoid the accusation of 'dualism', or believing in a second evil deity equal to God, by making it clear that the Devil was God's Ape: a creature who could do nothing but what he was ordered and permitted by God himself. Here we have the idea of the deserving demoniac: the possession victim who was morally unclean and therefore invited the Devil into himself.

Within this framework, the Devil's role as tempter was critical. Why else would a loving God permit the Devil to work evil on his chosen people, than to test their worthiness or give them the opportunity to show their courage and purity? Calvin took the fact that since the Devil's fall was not depicted in any great detail in the Bible, then his fall was not meant to be particularly useful or instructive to us. Instead, he noted that, "The tendency of all that scripture teaches us concerning devils is to put us on our guard against their wiles and machinations... the object of these descriptions is to make us more cautious and vigilant…"[4]

English Protestants took very much the same view. In 1537 Hugh Latimer wrote, "…as a sum of all we have experienced, the devil [is] a stinking sentine of all vice; a foul filthy channel of all mischiefs", with Thomas Cranmer writing that Satan's powers were, "without number and increase daily more and more… sadness, sorrow, trouble of conscience, faintness of heart, sickness of the body, poverty, slanders, despising, reproaches, persecutions, battle, sedition, hunger, pestilence and all plagues."[5]

The breadth of Satan's power and presence, from negative emotion to the source of bad thoughts to the cause of physical disease, would have put him at the centre of the Early Modern Londoner's life, whether they believed in the possibility of a physical manifestation of the Devil and demons or not. As we have seen, to Reginald Scott, arch sceptic and writer of *The Discoverie of Witchcraft*, devils and spirits existed; he merely disputed the physical manifestation of the ones cited in the books of demonologists.

Devils in Everyday Life

Thus, for the Protestant, the Devil was ever-present. Protestant Reformers like John Bale not only linked Protestant thinking to ancient writings within the Christian church – a possible reason why English Protestant thinkers were quite so wedded to Church Fathers like Augustine – but the belief in millenarianism, the idea that humanity was living through the last days, gave writers like Bale the chance to trace back through the lineage of the Church and 'pinpoint' the exact moment that Christianity had been infiltrated by the Antichrist. After all, the books of Revelation, and of Daniel, had warned of Satan's machinations. These theologians argued, perhaps disingenuously, that the Catholic Church was not just wrong, it was a corrupt branch of the faith in the service of the Devil.

This Satanic infiltration, though, wasn't the literal presence of the Devil depicted in Witches' Sabbats, like the lurid images of the Sabbat at North Berwick Kirk where witches supposedly ran around taking pieces of corpses and the Devil himself preached from the pulpit. This was a far more pervasive influence that represented an influence in every human life. As William Perkins wrote in his *Damned Art of Witchcraft*, "…Satan applies himself to man's measure and at his own will, draws the mind into error by his delusions and impostures."[6]

The English Protestant was not exorcised of Satan's influences the way a Catholic might be. His or her baptism would instead contain the promise to fight eternally against the works of Satan. Bishop Edwin Sandys noted in 1574, "so soon as we profess to be Christ's soldiers, as malicious and fierce enemy he invadeth us", while Perkins noted, "forgiveness of Sins and grievous temptation be inseparable companions to life"; and Latimer wrote, "The Devil knoweth all ways how to tempt us… insomuch that we can begin or do nothing, but that he is at our heels and worketh some mischief." Thomas Cranmer wrote similarly, writing in his *Catechismus* of the "sudden and vehement motions to do evil" that might appear at the Devil's bidding.[7]

Even the most mentally stable individual, with the benefit of modern psychiatry and solid self-esteem, has probably experienced troubling and intrusive thought. Negative ideas and impulses come upon us that can seem alien, thrust in from the outside. For the Early Modern Londoner, this was evidence of the continuing influence of the Devil, proving his reality by the commonality of experience. Stephen Gosson, a former playwright who turned minister, wrote, "…the Devil stands at our elbow when we see him not, speaks when we hear him not, strikes when we feel not, and woundeth sore when he raiseth no skin or rents the flesh."[8]

William Perkins, with perhaps a little less flair, wrote similarly, "[the Devil] conveys into a man's mind, either by inward suggestion or outward object, the motion or cognition of that sin which he would have him to commit."[9]

That ideas such as these had entered English drama were certain. Not only in the spectacle of Faust's good and bad angels fighting for his soul, but in this scene from *The Witch of Edmonton*, where the demon in the shape of a dog influences Frank Thornly to kill his lover Susan:

DOG: Now for an early mischief and a sudden!
The mind's about it now; one touch from me
Soon sets the body forward
[Enter FRANK and SUSAN]
FRANK: Your request
Is out; yet will you leave me?
SUSAN: What? So churlishly?
You'll make me stay for ever,
Rather than part with such a sound from you.
FRANK: Why you almost anger me. Pray you
be gone.
You have no company, and 'tis very early;
Some hurt betide you homewards.
SUSAN: Tush! I fear none;
To leave you is the greatest hurt I can suffer:
Besides, I expect your father and mine own
To meet me back, or overtake me with you;
They begin to stir when I came after you
I know they'll not be long.

FRANK: So! I shall have more trouble, –
[THE DOG RUBS AGAINST
HIM] – thank you for that:
[ASIDE] Then I'll ease all at once. It is done
Now;
What I ne'er thought on. – You shall not go back.
SUSAN: Why, shall I go along with thee? Sweet music!
FRANK: No, to a better place.
SUSAN: Any place I;
I'm there at home where thou pleasest to have me.
FRANK: At home? I'll leave you in your last
lodging;
I must kill you.
-- Act 3, Scene 3, The Witch of Edmonton, William
Rowley, Thomas Dekker and John Ford, (1621)

The Body of a Demon

When the Devil Pug comes from hell, he inhabits the body of a thief newly hanged at Tyburn. We can see a reason for this quoted in George Gifford's 1587 book, *A Discourse of the Subtill Practises of Devilles, Witches and Sorcerers*: he writes, "Our Saviour Christ saith that a spirite hath neither flesh nor bones. A spirit hath a substance, but yet such as in invisible, whereupon it must needs be graunted that Divels in their own nature have no bodily shape, nor visible forme, moreover it is against the truth, and against pietie to believe, that Divels can create or make bodies, or change one body into another for those things are proper to God. It followeth therefore that whensoever they appeare in a visible forme, it is no more but an apparition and counterfeit shewe of a bodie, unless a body be at any time lent them..."[10]

This idea that the body of a demon was insubstantial came from the works of early church thinkers like Augustine, whose philosophy was profoundly influential well into the Englightenment. Augustine held of demons, "The gods occupy the loftiest region, men the lowest, the demons the middle region. For the abode of the gods is heaven, that of men the earth, that of the demons the air." Augustine took the idea that demons occupied the air, and had bodies fashioned of it: "if they are aerial in body, in this they are alone... being aerial in body, how much value is to be set on that, since a soul of any kind whatsoever is to be set above every body?"[11]

This was a simplification of the theories of the 3rd century philosopher Porphyry, who followed the Classical idea of an element called Pneuma, which was partially airy, but partially liquid: an ethereal fluid that rippled and reacted to the stimuli around it. A contemporary, Origen, also believed in the idea that demons had a non-physical body, suggesting that demons needed sacrificial smoke from animals to embody themselves or fatten up their already existing airy forms.

This entirely suited Protestant sceptics like Reginald Scott, who wrote scornfully of witches with physically embodied imps or devils, "all divels, which were wont to be spirituall, may at their pleasure become corporall, and so shew themselves familiarlie to witches and conjurors…"[12]

Sceptics like Scott, the German Weyer, and the Londoner Jonson, utterly rejected the idea of corporeal demons, or those with any power to embody, and it's a clear message of Fitzdotterel's ignorance and fantasism (and implied Popery) that he expects his demon to appear with cloven hooves or in any way physically. However, that wasn't to say that while Jonson probably didn't believe in them, Protestant authorities didn't leave a window open for demons to interfere in the corporeal world.

Calvin, Luther and Transforming Ghosts into Demons

There had long been a link between ghosts and demons. The airy form of a demon allowed it to enter the cavities of the body and torment humans, but while it could make a living human being terribly ill, the soul present in the body would fight the demon for full control. This was why the Puritan tradition of bolstering the spirit with prayer and fasting, as was Biblical precedent, had the power to drive demons out by strengthening the native soul of the afflicted demoniac. The power of a soul over a demon was, again, sacrosanct: Augustine had written of the hierarchy of the fiery, celestial soul over the airy, 'aetherial' body of the demon.

The living human body was a vehicle of earth with a spirit of fire, but the dead body was an empty vessel with nothing to guard it. The works of the reformer Martin Luther had long held that the so-called ghost or spook was simply Satan in disguise, trying to tempt the unwary Christian into sinning by having masses said for the dead – a common Catholic practice for those suffering in purgatory, and a common trope in Pre-Reformation Christian ghost stories.

In his 1521 pamphlet, *The Misuse of Mass*, Luther wrote, "[Geister] are not the souls of men but simply devils who act and speak as if one could redeem them…", going on in one of his sermons to say, "If you have in your house a spook or ghost… it is the work of Satan. No soul has yet since the beginning of the world reappeared on the earth, and it is not God's will that it should be so."

Thus, if a ghost was seen, or if a ghost seemed to appear in a necromancer's magic circle – as Samuel had seemed to do in the Biblical story of the Witch of Endor – it was simply a demon in human form, something that would be worth considering for interpretations of Shakespeare's *Hamlet*.

More directly, for Jonson and his 1616 audience, there was direct authority from the King, in his 1597 book *Daemonologie*, that demons could inhabit the bodies of the dead. When his character Philomath asks Epistimon, "And will God them permit these wicked spirits to trouble the rest of a dead body before the resurrection thereof?" Epistimon replies, "What more is the rest troubled of a dead body: when the devil carries it out of the grace to serve his turn for a space… the devil may well use as well the ministry of the bodies of the faithful in these cases as of the unfaithful, there is no invonvenient: for his haunting the bodies after they are dead can in no-ways defile them, in respect of the soul's absence…"[13]

Sermon Tales and the Reinforcing of the Undead as Demons

The idea of the dead body as a waiting and convenient vehicle for the demonic joyrider had a solid Medieval provenance. While Reformers had sought to root out traces of Medievalism in many respects of their doctrines, their attitude to witches and ghosts often retained a curiously Medieval influence.

We see this in James' continentally influenced attitude to demons. It harks back to a story left by Thomas of Cantimpre. In his *De Bonum Universale de Apibus*, he wrote of a blessed virgin going to prayer during a night where the body of a local man was still lying in state at the local church. The Devil saw her in prayer, unafraid of either the corpse or the darkness, and became jealous. Angry, he inhabited the body and had it sit up, but the virgin was still unafraid, saying, "Lie down, lie down you wretch, for you have no power against me!"

The Devil, angered even further, sat up wearing the corpse and said, "Truly, I will have power over you, and I will revenge myself for the frequent injuries I have suffered at your hands!"

The holy virgin, showing her bravery, serenity, and sanctity, took a staff topped with a cross and caved the corpse's skull in, rendering the body useless to the Devil.

In the *Life of Ida of Louvaine*, the chronicler wrote about a vision where she saw a body on a funeral mound; the Devil then stepped into the corpse and animated it to attack the blessed virgin, while the Dominican Jean de

Mailly tells of a demon inhabiting the body of a beautiful young girl, recently deceased, who attempted to seduce a pious man.[14]

Therefore, we can see that even if Shakespeare, Marlowe and Jonson's audience weren't familiar with the precise stories retold here, they would certainly have been familiar with the idea of a demon inhabiting a dead body and wearing it for a few days.

In the 13th century theologian Thomas of Cantimpré's allegorical work, *De Bonum Universale de Apibus*, he describes the mechanism by which a corpse may become a vehicle for a Devil:

"Since the structure of a dead body remains behind, just as a man can use a structured body like a garment, so the Devil can sneak into it and can mould the mouth to voices and words again, and recall the tendons to the movement of its members."[15]

Enchanted by His Wife

Also relevant to Jonson's mentions of Simon Forman and his portrayal of the Renaissance Magus, is the scene in Act 5 of *The Devil is an Ass* where Merecraft and Everill are trying to persuade Fitzdotterel to fake possession against his wife, and therefore get out of legal difficulties by pretending a spirit has been sent to possess him. This discredits her as a witch, or at least someone who consorted with those who committed acts of black magic, and portrays Fitzdotterel as conveniently non-compos-mentis so far as any legal repercussions went for his actions.

This is a story that the 1616 audience of *The Devil is an Ass* would have been very familiar with. Only a few months before the play had been performed, London had been abuzz with the scandalous goings-on in the life of Lady Frances Carr, formerly Lady Frances Devereux, Countess of Essex. Lady Frances had been on trial for the murder of Sir John Overbury – a poet and writer – by poisoning in 1613, while he had been imprisoned in the Tower for displeasing the King.

Sir John had fallen foul of Lady Frances after writing the poem, *A Wife*, criticising her to his friend Robert Carr, the Earl of Somerset. Carr was also James VI's favourite at the time, and Frances was easily able to manipulate the unfortunate (and not well liked) Overbury into appearing disrespectful to Queen Anne, prompting the King to offer him an embassy to Russia, which he refused.

Jonson had already written of the fall of the Somersets, in his *Masque Golden Age Restored*, a performance of which had been attended by Lady Frances' ex-husband, the 3rd Earl of Essex, Robert Devereux. Here, the story of the paranoid, touchy and foolish Fitzdotterel being cuckolded and legally shamed by his beautiful wife finds its mirror in the real world.

While Essex was a conspicuously manly man – sporting a fine calf and a nice, full beard; a regular and incorrigible fighter and duellist – his marriage to Frances had been annulled by special dispensation in 1613, due to a purported inability to consummate with his beautiful wife. The pair had been married by arrangement when Devereux had been 14 years old and Frances 13, but had been immediately separated to prevent them from sex and conception too early, which was felt to be dangerous to health.

Unfortunately, while Essex had been away on a grand tour of Europe, his wife became infatuated with Robert Carr, one day to become the Earl of Somerset. Carr had become James' favourite after catching the King's eye while accidentally injuring himself during a royal hunt, and cut a more romantic figure in Frances' eyes than Devereux. In fact, during his earliest appearances at court the Earl of Suffolk had complained that some men were actually encouraging the King's favourite to flirt with their wives in the hope that it would get them noticed by the King.

However their courtship began, it would seem that Carr's interest in Frances was more than just casual. Even while his friend Overbury was writing letters begging him not to marry Frances, he reminisced about the time of Carr and Frances' falling in love, possibly with assistance from the poet Overbury.

However, Frances was still trapped in marriage with Essex and could not avoid him forever. In the winter of 1611 he took his wife to his estate in Staffordshire and kept her there with the purported intention of consummating the marriage and no longer being a cuckold. This was a sphere in which an Early Modern woman was, sadly, disempowered. Although Frances had no desire for sex with her husband by arranged marriage she would have no help in law if he should have taken her by force. Worst of all, her letters show a terrible fear that submitting to sex with Essex, whether voluntarily or not, would drive away Carr's suit for her and leave her bereft in a loveless marriage.

Even before then, Frances had taken a step that would later come back to haunt her: she had turned to Cunning Folk. Also called 'White Witches' and a number of other, less complimentary, names, Cunning Folk were magico-medical practitioners who had often educated themselves in a mixture of outdated medical practices: folk magic, grimoire magic and home-made remedies. The tradition of Cunning Folk aiding the political ambitions of nobility was far from new: in 1324 the Cunning Woman Margery Jourdemayne, known as the 'Witch of Eye', had been burned at the stake for supplying potions and spells to Eleanor Cobham, the Duchess of Gloucester. As late as 1682 the widespread use of Cunning Folk as potion brewers and fortune tellers in Paris would result in a huge, city-wide poisoning scare that saw the torture and death of dozens.

Forman seems to have had a characteristically affectionate relationship with Frances, as was his way. While she had romantic eyes only for Carr – at that time the Viscount Rochester – she wrote to Forman, "I still crave your love, although I hope I have it, I shall deserve it better hereafter, Your affectionate loving daughter", with the future Countess of Hertford openly calling Foreman, "Father."

One of Forman's largest sources of clientele was love matters. Frances' friend Anne Turner, arrested in 1615, had paid him to get her the affection of Sir Arthur Mainwaring, but had only succeeded in inducing a brief haze of lust where he had ridden through a storm at night to make love to her. We don't know precisely what he did for Frances, but when investigators searched his study after his death they found parchments inscribed with the seals of demons that they said were to vex Mainwaring and Carr if their affections towards his clients should wane. And we know that Forman had dabbled in necromancy to boost the signal of his astrology, although never to his own satisfaction.

Forman's skill in love magic didn't end at inflaming passion: he also supplied charms to prevent undesirable men from pestering their wives for sex. Frances herself wrote that he had supplied her with a number of 'jellies' for the magical purpose of either inflaming Carr or disabling Essex. Likewise, in one of his magical diaries he makes note of a spell involving a handkerchief to prevent a man from bothering a woman with lustful advances.

After Forman died in 1611, predicting his own illness and death a few days before, Frances sought to replace him with a series of increasingly disreputable figures: first the partnership of Gresham and Savoy, and then Mary Woods. In fact, it was when Anne Turner was arrested as an accessory to Overbury's murder, that she confessed that Savoy had supplied them with poison to kill Overbury, and had "practised many sorceries upon the Earl of Essex's person," and had attempted to blackmail Turner over her spells she had cast to get Mainwaring to marry her.

This narrative actually suited the Earl of Essex. Frances' father, Sir Thomas Howard, had pressed the idea of a suit of nullity on him, but Essex had been reluctant to agree to a scenario that presented him as incapable of his manly duties, which would prevent him from marrying in future. With the whisper that he had been enchanted, Essex's agreement to the nullity (with certain concerns) was easier, although he sent the investigators a 'certain round and hot letter' that was sadly destroyed.

This wasn't helped by the fact that in 1613, during the debate for the nullity at Lambeth Palace, the Cunning Woman Mary Woods was arrested and told a lurid story of Frances paying her with a £60 gold ring for, "a poison that would lay in a man's body three or four days… to be given to the Earl of Essex." Although Frances was not prosecuted at the time, the case of witchcraft was such an undertone in the debate that when George Abbot, the Archbishop of Canterbury, wrote on his disbelief in witchcraft, the King sent him a detailed and angry letter restating their power.[16]

Darrel, Harsnett and Fake Exorcism

In Act 5, Scene 3 of *The Devil is an Ass*, a scene takes place between Merecraft, Fitzdotterel and Everill where the ne'er do wells coach the hapless Fitzdotterel in 'little Darrel's tricks' for faking demonic possession, so that he can escape the consequences of the scheme he has become embroiled in.

'Little Darrel' was in fact the Puritan preacher John Darrel, a BA and former law student who had begun a career dispossessing demoniacs in the North of England, amongst various Puritan communities. Darrel was one of a trend of unlicensed preachers, not officially ordained, whom the mainstream Church had been keen to quash, leading to Darrel's 1599 trial at the hands of the Bishop of London's chaplain, Samuel Harsnett.

Darrel had been a bright and ambitious scholar, that we know: he attended Queens' College Cambridge as a sizar – a poor student on a scholarship – which would have required him to earn his scholarship money by waiting on tables for the fee paying students and reading the Bible aloud during meals. Sizars were also expected to excel academically and behave impeccably, with study being especially important considering that their scholarships constrained them from taking more than four years to complete their degrees.

Harsnett was a Northerner like Darrel, as was the Bishop of London Richard Bancroft, both from middle class backgrounds. Harsnett had shown Puritan tendencies in his early twenties, but had become a loyal worker against the Puritan cause. The mainstream Church had grave concerns over the Puritan love of decentralised, grassroots worship, with church policy being set at regular 'Prophesyings', where Puritan ministers would worship, preach, and debate doctrine. At a time when the Church of England was still seeking, as it had sought for some time, to centralise worship, these unregulated ministers and their anti-clerical rhetoric presented a growing threat.

The first wave of anti-Puritan persecutions had been against the Marprelate Press, a secret press sending out Puritan penned satires attacking Church of England policies. After Bancroft and Harsnett had infiltrated the Martinist groups and sent a number of writers either to prison or to the gallows; then came possession.

While the mainstream view promoted by the Church was that the age of miracles was over, and therefore wonders could not occur, Puritans, or The Godly, as they called themselves, maintained that demonic possession wasn't a miraculous thing, it was simply a method, like witchcraft, for God to demonstrate his wonder. The conspicuous power of the preacher and his congregation to drive out a demon using prayer and fasting was, for The Godly, tacit proof that theirs was the right path, and superior to either the mystically disarmed Church of England or the superstitious and ritualistic Catholic faith.

Darrel's first case had been an abortive attempt at dispossessing Katherine Wright in 1586. This fitted the mould that we would see again and again with possession cases in the Early Modern era – a girl or woman was possessed and accused another of sending a spirit to torment her by witchcraft. This is probably the case we know least about, since the justice overseeing the case appears to have been a staunch sceptic and had thrown the whole matter out, threatening Darrel with imprisonment. In her work on Darrel, Marion Gibson also says that even the wealthy patron who brought him into the case lost faith half way through and publicly rejected his assistance.

Despite the failure of Darrel's involvement with Katherine Wright, he was still influential enough to be brought into the case of Thomas Darling ten years later. We cannot know whether Darrel was involved in attempted dispossessions of other afflicted Godly Parishioners. Aside from a rather cold list of deaths and births – Darrel had buried his parents and fathered five children, one of whom had died and two of whom appear only in Darrel's personal writing – we know little about how Darrel spent the years between 1586 and 1596.

Thomas Darling's possession, like the possessions of the women Nicole Obry and Marthe Brossier in France earlier that century, had started seemingly as an attempt at a 'good' possession where the boy preached the 'good word' and described 'green angels' at the window. Before Godly exorcists got involved, Thomas' narrative was one almost of martyrdom:

"How he spent the time between his fits, it is worth observing. His exercises were such as might well have befitted one of riper years, wherein he showed the fruits of his education, which was religious and godly. With those that were good Christians he took great pleasure to confer. To them he would signify his daily expectation of death, and his resolute readiness to leave the world and to be with Christ."[17]

After a local saddler and preacher Jessee Bee had spoken with the boy's aunt, asking whether he had been bewitched, Darling had told a story of how he had met Alice Gooderige, a local woman, in the woods and had offended her by breaking wind, leading to her cursing him.

Darling's possession took shape very much like the possession of the London lawyer Robert Brigges – the Devil tempted him and tormented him, and he narrated the whole thing for the crowds watching him. Darling's main dispossessor at the start of the case was a local minister Arthur Hildersham, but Darrel seems to have become involved when a copy of the case was sent to him for publication.

Darrel had suggested that the spirit should be driven out according to a line from Matthew 17:21, "Howbeit this kind goeth not out but by prayer and fasting", but refused to become involved personally for fear of being accused of vainglory, possibly after having been burned by the affair of Katherine Wright. The next day the boy's family and friends had gathered as Darrel had suggested and the boy declared himself dispossessed, narrating a battle between the word of God and his trio of possessed demons.

The 'Seven at Lancashire' were the members of the Starkie household, first possessed, and then sexually assaulted and blackmailed by the Cunning Man Edmund Hartley, who was eventually hanged after pestering a poor relation of the family named Margaret Byron and following her home.

The case that Jonson finished with, though, was that of William Sommers in Nottingham. It was the case that gave Darrel the closest thing he got to recognition: during the battles with Sommers the demoniac, the people of Nottingham installed Darrel as a regular preacher, although the local clergy complained that he spoke of nothing but demoniacs.

Unfortunately, Sommers' demon got the better of them: in identifying witches, he accused Alice Freeman, a cousin of the alderman and Justice of the Peace William Freeman. Understanding the legal issues at stake – Alice Gooderidge at Burton and Hartley in Lancashire had both hanged on the word of demoniacs – the Freeman camp immediately accused Sommers of witchcraft and had him arrested, where he admitted to pretending his fits. While the Darrel camp could well have pressured Sommers to withdraw his claims, as he seems to have done, this was the beginning of the end.

The Archbishop of York set up a commission, which brought Samuel Harsnett to the North. In the meantime, Sommers had vacillated between admitting fraud and claiming to be genuine – claiming his fits were genuine on March 20th, and then not only admitting fraud to the mayor and justices on March 31st, but also demonstrating his fits before them.

In fear of violent clashes – the townspeople, already divided, argued vociferously over whether Sommers was a harassed demoniac or a wavering fake – the Archbishop of Canterbury took decisive action. Sommers, Wright, the Lancashire victims, Darling, Darrel and Darrel's co-exorcist More were all imprisoned in London.

During these interrogations Sommers narrated a passage that bears a striking resemblance to Merecraft's coaching of Fitzdotterel. He said of Darrel:

"I will teach thee to doe all those trickes which Katherine Wright did, and many others that are more straunge. Besides (quoth he) if thou wilt so doe, thou shalt neuer want whilest thou liuest. Hereunto when I had agreed, he told me more particularly what the said

Katherine Wright did at seuerall times, in her fittes: as that she foamed at the mouth, gnashed with her teeth: cryed and scritched, catched & snatched at those that stood by her, (especially at him the said M.Darrell): laughed out of measure: fell into great shewes of sadnesse: wallowed and tumbled: cast her selfe into the fire, and sometimes into the water: would lie as though she had been sencelesse: and many other things M.Darrell then told me: saying, that I might learne to doe them very easily. And the better to teach me, hee did thereupon himselfe, acte diuers of them. For gnashing with his teeth, he knocked his own teeth together diuers times. For foaming, he rolled his tongue in his mouth, & then put out some little spittle betwixt his lips: but said, that I might soone learne to doe it better, by rolling a stone in my mouth, but especially if I could get a little soape to vse at such times. Likewise he shewed with his hands halfe open, the manner of her snatching & catching, & for some other of her doings he shewed some other gestures."[18]

Harsnett, eager to provide a blast against the cohesion of the Godly community, published his record of Darrel's trial and fakery in his 1599 book, *A Discovery of the Fraudulent Practises of John Darrel*, which Jonson almost certainly would have read, as I suspect Shakespeare did. The scene that follows in Act 5, Scene 3 is a perfect reconstruction of the sceptic's view of the dispossession: a fake demoniac using magic tricks and rehearsed phrases of foreign languages to fool credulous onlookers:

MERECRAFT: It is the easiest thing, sir, to be done,
As plain as fizzling: roll but wi' your eyes,
And foam at th' mouth. A little castle-soap
Will do 't to rub your lips; and then a nut shell,

With tow, and touch-wood in it, to spit fire.
Did you ne'er rear, sir, little Darrel's tricks
With the boy o'Burton, and the seven in Lancashire,
Somers at Nottingham? All these do teach it.
And we'll give out, sir, that your wife has bewitched
you...
-- Act 5, Scene 3, The Devil is an Ass, Ben Jonson,
(1616)

To Harsnett the whole thing was theatre, and this is what makes *The Devil is an Ass* a strange Mobius strip of meta-theatre. It is a play that mentions itself and its own venue as existing in the universe the play takes place in, where a real devil stands by while a desperate fool pretends to be possessed so that he can enrich his con men. The perfect Jonson blast at both Puritanism and credulity.

Jonson, however, was not the only playwright with an interest in Puritan exorcists.

Harsnett, Bancroft, and Twelfth Night

In order to understand the relationship between Shakespeare's *Twelfth Night* and demonic possession, it is helpful to engage in a little conjecture about a possible first performance of the play, or at least whom Shakespeare might have spent his Christmas with.

In the papers of the Duke of Northumberland, discovered by the historian Leslie Hotson, is the following entry:

"1601/2, Jan 6. A full narrative or description of the reception and entertainment of the Muscovite ambassador and of an Italian nobleman, the Duke of Brachiana, who were received at the Court of Queen Elizabeth, together with the names of noblemen in attendance on her Majesty at her dining abroad upon Twelfth-day January 1601-2…"

The full text tells us very clearly who is present:

"*The Karver* The Earle of Sussex
The Cupbearer The Earle of Darbye
To cast the Surnap and take th'assay The Lord Thomas Howard, The Lord of Effingham
The Sewer The Lord Windsor
To cary the Trane The Lord Chamberlain, The Lord Cobham
The Earle of Worcester
The Earle of Rutland
The Earle of Cumberland *To give [...]*
To come before the meat
Admirall The Lord Steward
Lord Tresorer
The Comptroller
To followe the meat

All officers of househowlde
To say grace
The Lord Archbishop of Canterbury
The Lord Bisshop of London
The Lord Bisshop of Eely
The Lord Bisshop of Almoner
The Deane of York and all her Majesties chaplains…"[19]

The record fails to leave us with definitive proof that the play was either Shakespeare's or *Twelfth Night*. Certainly, we know that Ben Jonson's *Cynthia's Revels* was written in the hopes of being performed at the Court's Christmas revels, however the Lord Chamberlain's notes for January 6th 1601 show that Jonson's company, The Children of the Chapel, were performing a carol that night, as was traditional, rather than any sort of play. Furthermore, with such a varied audience and the high diplomatic stakes – Elizabeth was keen to impress her Italian and Russian guests – it would seem counter intuitive that she would prefer an acerbic satire like Jonson's *Revels* over the gentler, musical comedy of Shakespeare's *Twelfth Night*.

A memorandum from Lord Chamberlain Hunsdon, Shakespeare and Burbage's patron, states his intention to, "Confer with my Lord Admirall and the Master of the Revells for takeing order generally with the players to make choyse of play that shalbe best furnished with rich apparel, have greate variety and change of Musicke and daunces, and of a Subiect that may be most pleasing to her Maiestie." While there might be some alternative choice in the papers of the Lord Admiral's Men, either Hunsdon or the Lord Admiral choosing the difficult and presumptuous Jonson over their own companies would seem unlikely.

Having been played on Twelfth Night would certainly make more sense of the play's title. Faybyan's remark, "More matter for a May Morning" suggests that the play might well be located at that time, although Belch's bolstering remark to Aguecheek ("Were we not born under Taurus?") might be nothing more than a comical remark playing on astrologically determined personality stereotypes.

In either case, a debut on Twelfth Night at Court would certainly give the play more reason to be named *Twelfth Night* than its other known performance date: Candlemass at Middle Temple Hall. The diary of barrister John Manningham states, "At our feast wee had a play called 'Twelue Night, or What you Will,' much like the Commedy of Errores, or Menechmi in Plautus, but most like and neere to that in Italian called *Inganni*. A good practise in it to make the Steward beleeve his Lady widdowe was in love with him, by counterfeyting a letter as from his Lady in generall termes, telling him what shee liked best in him, and prescribing his gesture in smiling, his apparaile, &c., and then when he came to practise making him beleeue they tooke him to be mad."

With the Chamberlain's Men having taken the honour of performing at the Queen's prestigious seasonal revels for the four years leading up to 1601, it would be surprising for them to have been ousted. Although Henslow's diaries for May 1601 do show that Henslow took money from the Court for the Admiral's Men's involvement in Her Majesty's Christmas plays, there is no mention in his papers that the Admiral's Men had performed on Twelfth Night more recently than 1586 (there's also a strong suggestion that the Royal Court were monumentally slow payers).

However, having been played at court before that specific audience would give shape to the play in ways that would be critical: the proud Olivia as an allegory of Elizabeth's political position: independent, yet available; the Falstaff-like Sir Toby Belch (a favourite character type of the Queen's); the fortuitously named Duke Orsino... and critically, Malvolio.

Even more critically, at that time The Lord Bishop of London was Richard Bancroft, Samuel Harsnett's paymaster and a man who might have raised just as much of a smile over the comparisons between Shakespeare's hypocritical steward and the Puritans that Bancroft and Harsnett had been battling.

Malvolio the Puritan

As a woman whose life had been threatened and complicated by religious innovation, Elizabeth made no secret of her distaste for new developments in state religion. She had spent the largest portion of her life trying to ensure conformity to the Church of England. With Catholic conspiracies against her life following from the Pope's excommunication in 1570, Elizabeth's response to the Puritan movement, and their unwillingness to accept the centralised rule of the Church, had been brutal. With a rising Catholic threat, the state machine had been anxious to avoid fighting on two religious fronts. The Archbishop of Canterbury, Edmund Grindal, had been placed under house arrest for defending Puritan doctrinal meetings.

One critical voice in the battle was the 1588 pamphleteer who called himself 'Martin Marprelate'. Martin attacked the Church of England's ecclesiastical structure, demanding that the bishops be ejected from their palaces. Martin's pamphlets were scurrilous, satirical and irreverent, attacking the very core of the Church.

The response was the team of Archbishop Whitgift, Bishop Bancroft and Reverend Samuel Harsnett. Harsnett was an accomplished scholar and Bancroft's personal chaplain. He was a former student of Lancelot Andrews at Pembroke College and a skilled, if acerbic, writer. Bancroft was the one who put the plan into action: punishing Puritan sympathisers, raiding prayer groups, interrogating Puritans, seizing letters, spying on groups and infiltrating the Puritan community of London.

A Royal Commission against seditious religious books sent printers and authors to both prison and the gallows – with the Martinist author John Pendry being hanged in Southwark on May 29th 1592.

That Malvolio was meant to be portrayed as a Puritan is certain. Maria describes him as, "a kind of Puritan", snidely hinting at Puritan hypocrisy with the follow-up, "the devil a Puritan that he is, or anything constantly but a time-pleaser; an affectioned ass that cons state without book and utters it by great swathes".

Actors had a common enemy in Puritans. As much as the movement threatened the mainstream Church, it threatened the theatre in far more direct terms. Stephen Gosson's 1582 book, *Plays Confuted in Five Actions*, he writes, "that in Stage Playes for a boy to put one the attyre, the gesture, the passions of woman ... is by outwarde signes to shewe [himself] otherwise then [he is] .... The diuel is not ignorant how mightely these outward spectacles effeminate, & soften ye hearts of men, vice is learned with beholding, sense is tickled, desire pricked, and those impressions of mind are secretly conueyed ouer to ye gazers, which ye plaiers do counterfeit on ye stage."[20]

This mutual suspicion of Puritans shared by courtiers, churchmen, players, and probably a number of people in liberal society, had given rise to the late 16th century curse, "The Devil is a Puritan", put in the mouth of Feste.

However, Puritanism had reacted to Whitgift and co.'s persecution by turning inwards, so the Devil had become a staple in reaffirming the power of Puritan faith: demonic possession and exorcism. The play even contains a reference to a specifically Puritan exorcism: the Starkie children of Lancashire, possessed in 1595 and whose latest pamphlet was hot off the presses in 1600. As the Clown says, "Bibble Babble", we have a line from the 1600 pamphlet on Darrel's exorcism of the Lancashire Seven: "When we called for the Bible, they fell about laughing at it, and said, 'Reach them the bibble bable, bibble babbell.'"[21]

Malvolio in the Dark

Another key dialogue comes between Malvolio and the
Fool. Malvolio has been locked in a lightless dungeon,
while the Fool facetiously maintains that it is light
enough:

*FOOL: I'm Sir Topas the priest. I've come to visit
Malvolio*
the Lunatic.
*MALVOLIO: Sir Topas, Sir Topas, good Sir Topas, go to
my lady—*
*FOOL: Out, hyperbolical fiend! How vexest thou this
man!*
Talkst thou nothing but of ladies?
SIR TOBY BELCH: [ASIDE] Well said, Master Parson.
*MALVOLIO: Sir Topas, never was a man thus wronged.
Good Sir*
*Topas, do not think I am mad. They have laid me
here in hideous darkness.*
*FOOL: Fie! Thou dishonest Satan! I call thee by the
most modest*
*terms, for I am one of those gentle ones that
will use the devil himself with courtesy. Sayest thou
that house is dark?*
MALVOLIO: As hell, Sir Topas.
*FOOL: Why, it hath bay windows as transparent as
barricadoes, and the clerestories towards the south-
north are as lustrous as ebony. And yet complainest
thou of obstruction?*
*-- Act 4, Scene 2, Twelfth Night, William Shakespeare,
(1601–02)*

Blindness, or the deprivation of any of the senses, was
one of the most common of the symptoms of possession
amongst Puritan demoniacs. Writing in defence of John

Darrel, the Starkie children, known as the "Lancashire Seven", are thus described by George More, "Most of them were both blind, deaf and dumb for divers days together… they were out of their minds without the use of the senses…"[22]

Similarly, in 1590, Elizabeth Throckmorton is described as being in a demonic fit where her eyes were, "closed as though she was blind", and in another fit, "Being both dumb, deaf and blind."

Broadly speaking, there were two forms of demonic illness: obsession and possession. Possession was the demonic control from within: the demon speaking through the host as it did in the case of the Nottingham demoniac William Sommers or in the case of the Boy of Burton, Thomas Darling. Those who were truly possessed had taken the demon into their body: Augustine wrote that demons could enter the body through entryways as varied as the eyes, the mouth, the ears, the anus or even wounds. An overwhelmingly common way for the demons to enter the body was via the lungs or skin.

This came from another Augustinian idea – the classical idea that darkness was an ethereal fluid that hung in the air, and that this fluid contained demons. The demon, with its cold, wet, etheric body could hang in the darkness, or in the 'bad air' of unclean places, and possess the unwary victim. In *On the Divination of Demons*, Augustine had written, "using the subtlety of their bodies to penetrate the bodies of men without their feeling it, and intermingling themselves into their thoughts… through certain imaginative visions…"

With the mouth seen as the entrance to both body and soul, the demon could enter the body and move around the hollows and empty spaces within. Caesarius of Heisterbach, sermon writer and theologian, describes it in his *Dialogue on Miracles* in terms that are still in operation during the 16th and 17th century: "…the devil can live inside the body's open spaces and in the bowels where the *stercora* is contained."

Even after the performance of *Twelfth Night*, this idea of the demon travelling around inside the body has credence. In the 1615 account of the possession of Alexander Nyndge, his brother writes, "He was often seen to have a certain swelling or variable lump to a great bigness, swiftly running up and down between the flesh and the skin." The outed, and allegedly fake, demoniac William Sommers was observed in George More's 1598 work, *A Brief Narration*, where More writes of a lump, "…that would run in a variable size between the flesh and shin, up and down his body, from leg to leg, then to his toe, belly, ear, root cheek, throat, tongue and eye, changing the colour of the eye, making the part it was in inflexible and heavy as iron."[23] This is not unlike the French Catholic demoniac Nicole Obry, whose demon was temporarily vanquished by being driven into her left arm by the application of the host.

The possessing demon was not thought to be able to affect the soul directly. Medieval theologian Caesarius had felt that, "The devil cannot be inside a human soul… penetration into the mind is possible only for him who created it… the mind of a man cannot be filled, according to its substance, by anything other than the creator of the trinity."[24]

This conformed with the Augustinian idea that the Devil could enter the body and affect the mind with visions and deceit. The visionary nun Hildegard von Bingen wrote,

"[The devil] overshadows [the soul] and obscures it with shadows and the smoke of his blackness…; meanwhile the soul is as if sleepy and unaware what the flesh of its body is doing."

Then what does the demon do to the body once it has sung the mind to sleep? A huge part of the Devil's activities would seem to fit with Malvolio's fit of strangeness. Malvolio suddenly dresses in his yellow stockings cross-gartered – surprising and highly inappropriate for a man of his age in 17th century England – and makes improper suggestions to the Lady Olivia. The same vanity of dress seems to have afflicted the Lancashire demoniac Margaret Hurdman, who narrated visions of being offered beautiful, courtly clothing, "I will have a fine smock of silk, not of red but of the best silk that is. It will be embroidered a foot high. It will be laid on with gold lace. It will have a French body, not of whalebone for that is not stiff enough, but of horn for that will hold it out. It shall come low in the front to keep in my belly… I will have a French farthingale… I will have it low at the front and high behind, and broad on either side, that I may lay my arms on it…"[25]

The possessed were also frequently foul, and blasphemous. William Sommers is said to have attempted to mount a female dog during his possession, distorting the words of the Lord's Prayer, saying, "Lead us into Temptation" and speaking the Latin phrase, "EGO SUM REX, EGO SUM DEUS",[26] pronouncing that he was God and king. Likewise, as we shall examine again in Lancashire, seven possessed children – also dispossessed by Darrel – disrupt their attempted exorcism by "misnaming every word as far as we went in it. For when we perceived such horrible blasphemy, we dared not proceed."[27]

If the status of the demoniac as speaking on behalf of the Devil was ever in doubt, then the demon would sometimes speak directly from the place of its residence. This had been the case with the French Catholic demoniac, Nicole Obry, who had attracted record crowds during her public exorcisms at Leon in 1566. A light-voiced young girl, she had disputed with the bishop using a deep, rumbling voice that came from her belly.

The Puritan demoniacs exercised similar demonic voices. In the case of Thomas Darling, the Boy of Burton, he narrated three voices: one "a small voice" and two others, "speaking very hollowly, as both those unnatural voices not uttered by himself were." In the case of the outed demoniac William Sommers, his demonic voice, much like Obry's, circumvented even the use of his lips: "…he lay many times with his mouth extraordinarily void and strangely open. And he spoke these words… 'I will use WS's tongue and members for three days…' without moving or stirring his tongue or lips." We hear exactly the same accusation in Act 3, Scene 4 of *Twelfth Night*, where Maria says, "Lo, how hollow the fiend speaks within him!" In the case of the Starkie children in Lancashire, George More writes, "…such strangeness in their voices, that the uttering and framing of them exceeded all cunning intervention or the skill of any counterfeit imitation… the effect was also so fearful, that it was both terrible and troublesome to the whole country, and wrought a wonderful astonishment in all that heard it."

While the Protestant view of salvation was by no means universal, the influential Calvinist theory was one of predestination: the soul was either damned or saved and there was nothing that could be done about it. To accept the idea of being damned or saved was sin, and would mean you were damned, and the prevailing Calvinist belief was that many, if not most, were damned.

In the traditional Protestant view, possession came for one of two reasons: either because of a body's sinfulness or as a message from God so that all could be in awe of his glory. Christianity of the time was loath to ascribe any power whatsoever to the Devil himself. Satan was, as Martin Luther wrote, "God's Ape". A servant whose ill deeds were entirely part of the divine plan.

The proud and opportunistic Malvolio would be a prime candidate for possession as a punishment for sin. He is a humourless, self-important hypocrite – much the sort of person who Shakespeare and the orthodox clergy would have issue with in the anti-clerical, anti-theatre Puritan movement. We see the link between possession and sin in the 1615 possession of Alexander Nyndge, whose brother exhorted him, "If you earnestly repent of your sins, and pray to God for the forgiveness of the same, my life for yours, the Devil cannot hurt you." Even the outed pretender Rachel Pinder's demon stated that he had come to claim her because, "She has sinned against the Holy Ghost. And her sins were before her face, and he [the Devil] would have her."

If, then, possession represented the sins of the demoniac drawing the devil or demon inside, then what was obsession? Coined from the Latin word *obsessio*, a demoniac in obsession was one besieged by demonic entities rather than inhabited. Protestant writers tended to favour the term 'vexation', although both terms carried an implication of blamelessness.

Vexation was not the fault of the demoniac. Often, it was the malicious act of a neighbour. In the case of the Throckmorton children, whose possession lasted in the region of three years, the targets of blame were the Sampson family, in particular the elderly Agnes Sampson, of whom the girls said, "It is she… that has bewitched us, and she will kill us if you do not take her away."

Within the realm of the Puritan demoniacs, sorcerers were also usually to blame for the vexation of demoniacs. The anonymously written 1597 pamphlet about Thomas Darling describes his possession after offending the elderly Alice Gooderige, "That same Saturday that my sickness took me, I lost my uncle in the wood, and in the coppice I met a little old woman. She had a grey gown with a black fringe about the cape, a broad fringed hat, and three warts on her face. I have seen her begging out at door… as I passed by her in the coppice, I chanced, against my will, to pass wind which she, taking in anger, said, 'Gyp with a mischiefe and fart with a bell, I will goe to heaven and thou shalt goe to hell.'"[28]

Even William Sommers blamed his possession on an altercation with an old beggar woman who he met on the road to Nottingham who asked him for money and then supposedly forced him to eat a bewitched piece of bread and butter. Sommers also told another story of his bewitchment due to a then-dead woman from Worcestershire who had sent spirits to vex him because he had refused to give her his hatband.

The fact that Shakespeare doesn't include a witch, or even have Malvolio, in his desperation, invent one, could well just be a streamlining of plot.

Malvolio does not buy into the idea of being possessed, and therefore does not necessarily make comment on the cause of his affliction… however it DOES certainly place him in the position of either faker or sinner, rather than afflicted victim.

The Denham Exorcisms

Malvolio's position as demoniac and prisoner might also have been a reference to another hot topic of 1600 and 1601. In 1585, the wealthy Catholic Peckham family had been harbouring a number of Catholic priests. The priests were sheltered under assumed names and disguises to protect them from notice while they carried out the tasks expected of a priest in a wealthy household.

Also in the household was a young maid named Sarah Williams, and her sister Friswood, or Fid. Sarah had been told almost on her arrival that the house was "troubled with spirits", which spooked her no end, but also the girl was unable to pronounce the Latin devotions or make the various crosses required by the Peckham family's religion. By 1585, Protestants rarely, if ever, crossed themselves, believing the practice to be superstitious.

Matters came to a head one night when, during a thunderstorm, Sarah was too nervous to cross herself and stumbled over the words of the blessing she had been taught. Convicting someone as diabolical on the strength of stumbling over a prayer was far from a uniquely Catholic phenomena. In the case of the Starkie children, their enchanter, the Cunning Man Edmund Harltey, was examined by preachers and found to be a witch because, "he began to fumble around very ill-favouredly, and could not for his life say it to the end," when asked to recite the Lord's Prayer. In the case of Thomas Darling, the unfortunate Alice Gooderidge, who died while awaiting trial, also failed while attempting to speak the Lord's Prayer: "They caused her to say the Lord's

Prayer and the Creed, which she hurried through with much ado. But when she came to these words in the Lord's Prayer, 'and lead us not into Temptation', and in the Creed to 'Jesus Christ', 'The Holy Ghost', or 'The Catholic Church', she would not say any of those words."

For the clandestine priest Father Dibdale, this wasn't a sign that Sarah was a witch, but it was a sign that the Devil was at work within her. He first demanded that she be baptised into the Catholic faith and stop attending Protestant church, which she obeyed. Unfortunately, Sarah simply could not learn the Catholic blessing.

This tipped Sarah, her sister Fid and five others into a catch-22 world of demonism and exorcism. Just as the Clown facetiously takes everything Malvolio says as further evidence that he is possessed, so did the growing number of Catholic exorcists take everything that their charges said as evidence of possession. Every act, from admitting possession to denying it and the tiniest error made while praying, confirmed the demoniac's possession. For the next eight months, the girls were prisoners, until the extremes reached during exorcisms drew such great disapproval even from other Catholics, that the clerics were arrested, tried and hanged.

By 1598, the Catholic agent Robert Barnes had been arrested and his *Miracle Book* fell into the hands of the authorities, triggering a brief inquiry into the case in 1599, where the demoniacs were re-interviewed. This sign of Catholic disunity amongst the waning hidden enemy in England was something that the anti-possession Bancroft encouraged. Rome had attempted to bring order back to the schism between secular priests and the Jesuits by installing Robert Blackwell to the position of "Archpriest" over England and Scotland, but without direct authority over the Jesuits.

The attempt failed. Even by 1601 the volley of recriminatory pamphlets had started, and the rumblings of a schism between Catholics must have been on the lips of anyone in the know. Richard Bancroft, Whitgift's favoured hitman when it came to unruly sectarians, was at the centre of it. The Jesuits feared that weakening the influence of Rome in England would weaken English Catholicism… and Bancroft agreed wholeheartedly.

With the Privy Council's backing, Bancroft started to give support to the secular pamphleteers. Two of them, Watson and Bluet, even spent some time at his palace in Fulham. The book by his right hand man, his chaplain Samuel Harsnett, was an important part of that. Published two years after *Twelfth Night*, but certainly influential on *King Lear*, Harsnett penned, *A Declaration of Certain Egregious Popish Impostures*, a direct attack on Catholic William Weston, whom it characterised as an instrument of Jesuit interference.

Harsnett's delight at picking apart the Catholic arguments in the *Miracle Book* is evident in the exuberance that he brings to *A Declaration*. With the presses firing up to bring the archpriest schism to full fruition, the story of the Denham exorcism would have doubtless been in the public consciousness, not least the consciousness of Shakespeare, who seems to have liked a good exorcism.[29]

Harsnett and Bancroft

If Bancroft was Archbishop Whitgift's anti-Puritan, anti-Catholic, anti-mysticism axe man, then who was his chaplain, Samuel Harsnett?

He was the son of a Colchester baker, born in Farnsworth, Lancashire. Like William Shakespeare, his family were reasonably well off, with his grandmother leaving a house to her children. When Harsnett's cousin Adam Halsnoth died, he left the not inconsiderable sum of £160.

His education had started at the local grammar school. A local ecclesiastical lawyer named Bridgewater put him through school at Dedham, a centre for Calvinism, and there are hints at strong Protestantism, if not Puritanism, in Harsnett's youth.

Unlike William Shakespeare though, Harsnett's education had continued to university level. He entered the Kings' College, Cambridge, on September 8th 1576 with his patron's son, but migrated to Pembroke Hall in 1580 and only actually achieved his BA there, holding a scholarship that led to a fellowship, and in 1584, an MA by seniority. Here he was at the centre of the battle for English Protestantism: the catechist was Lancelot Andrews, a staunch anti-Calvinist, and the master: William Fulke, a famous Puritan.

By Harsnett's early career he was already controversial. He was sent before the High Commission for refusing to wear a surplice, which he unashamedly admitted. This suggested him to be very much in the anti-vestment camp of the Puritan Fulke, and might even have seen prison because of his commitment, before returning briefly to his native Colchester as a schoolmaster, although the school was not able to hold him for long.

By 1594, Harsnett was back at Pembroke College and was the leader of the anti-Calvinist faction, making a powerful attack on the doctrine of predestination at St. Paul's Cross. By 1595, his patron was Francis Bacon, and when Bancroft's career took him to the Bishopric of London in 1597, Harsnett was made his chaplain, swiftly installed at an ecclesiastical living in Chigwell.

Richard Bancroft was of a similar background to Harsnett. He was the son of gentry from Farnsworth, and had progressed from the local grammar school to Christ's College, Cambridge. Sometime around 1575, when the sheriff had applied to Cambridge University for a preacher to attend the assize courts, the authorities sent Bancroft. During his stay, Bancroft found a Puritan-penned libel against the Queen hung in a local church at Bury, and investigated, leading to the capture and conviction of two men, greatly ingratiating himself with his patrons.

Bancroft's name as an anti-Puritan cleric seems to have spread from there: in 1585 the anti-Puritan nobleman Sir Christopher Hatton gifted Bancroft a benefice, and he was made the Treasurer of St. Paul's. Other jobs followed, based most often on Bancroft's talent for rooting out radical elements within the Church and neutralising them. He preached against Puritans at St. Paul's Cross in 1588–89, and his 1593 book, *Dangerous Positions and Proceedings, Published and Practised within this Hand of Brytaine, and A Survay of the Pretended Holy Discipline* was a hammerblow to English Puritans, portraying them as treasonous and unreliable.

By 1596, Bancroft had been of sufficient use to Whitgift that he advanced him as the new Bishop of London to Elizabeth, a position that he initially lost out on to Richard Fletcherfor all of nine months, before Bancroft was sworn in on May 9th, 1597. Frank Walsh Brownlow says that Fletcher was described as a "comfy and courtly prelate". Bancroft might have been courtly, but he was certainly not comfortable. Considering the political climate in the late 1590s and early 1600s, a 'comfy' prelate was probably not required. The two men had met through Bancroft's investigations of the Marprelate affair, which had taken them on a winding route of investigation from the halls of Cambridge, to Dedham, outside Colchester.

When the former law student and unlicensed preacher John Darrel had become a symbol for Puritan exorcism in Lancashire and Nottingham, Harsnett was the obvious man to back Bancroft's campaign. While the Church orthodoxy held that the world had run dry of miracles and that all prophesy and revelation was finished now that the scriptures were revealed, exorcism, and even witchcraft, represented a problem. If demoniacs were sincere, then what power did the Orthodox Church have against them? What was more, did this mean that Puritan ministers had more power, and a greater mandate from God, than the mainstream Anglican faction?

Darrel was a dangerous symbol for the Puritan movement, and a threat to the Church. Exorcism offered tangible proof of God's existence. Since the Medieval era, demoniacs had been interrogated for tales of heaven and hell. Despite Luther and Calvin's protestations that the Devil was the father of lies and incapable of speaking any worthwhile revelation, surely if the Devil and his minions existed, so did God? If the unlicensed Darrel and his colleagues could drive out the manifest Devil, surely that showed their holiness. The Puritan exorcism was no popish ceremonial burlesque – their work took its cue directly from the Bible: prayer and fasting would drive the Devil out, and so Puritan congregations fasted and prayed along with their preachers, coming together as a whole in order to drive the Devil from the midst.

When Lord Chief Justice Anderson had informed Bancroft of trouble in the North in 1598, the Bishop of London moved into ruthless action. By now, the demoniac William Sommers had confessed to fraud in front of the Nottingham aldermen, where Darrel had been legitimised with a preaching position.

Bancroft had Sommers brought to his London house and questioned under an assumed name. Notes and pamphlets about the Starkies, Darling and another demoniac called Katherine Wright were examined and Harsnett despatched to the North to investigate. Commissions were set up in Nottingham, Derbyshire, and Leicestershire, with Harsnett sitting on a second commission at Nottingham.

Harsnett's method of attack was not unlike Shakespeare's: he used humour and his erudite sense of the ridiculous against the serious, highbrow prose of the Puritans. His skills in investigation showed through his almost forensic analysis of their texts, and his finely tuned abilities when interrogating suspects. Harsnett shows a rich inner life when writing his books against exorcism. He writes using the language of sport, likening the Puritans to foxes. He also uses the language of the stage and theatre to describe the whole environment of the exorcist and demoniac.

Harsnett had another thing in common with Shakespeare: both men would fall into trouble for their connections with the Essex rebellion. Shakespeare, who wrote plays in the language of the common citizen, and Harsnett, who wrote his critiques using the language of the hunt, both made unwise publications. For Shakespeare it was his performing and writing of *Richard II*, a play connected with the ancestor by which Essex claimed right of accession to the throne. For Harsnett, it was allowing the publication of John Hayward's *The First Part of the Life and Rainge of King Henrie IIII*, dedicated to Essex and dealing favourably with the deposition of Richard II.

Whether the two men commiserated or not, Shakespeare's portrayal of foolish demoniacs and dissembling false priests like the Clown in *Twelfth Night*, shows a familiarity with, if not a taste for Harsnett's work; Shakespeare's *King Lear* contains direct quotes from Harsnett's book of 1603.

The Middle Temple

Even Shakespeare's second performance might well
have found an audience receptive to a little humour on
the topic of demonic possession. As Manningham's
diary states, *Twelfth Night* was certainly performed on
February 2nd 1601, before the lawyers and students of
Middle Temple.

The lawyers of the Inns of Court had a culture all to
themselves. Students arriving there were largely left to
their own devices to pursue their studies, and the
communities of the lawyers had a particular atmosphere,
attitude and even language (in the form of Latin and
legal jargon), that set them apart.

Perhaps because of this, the Inns took
to Protestantism slowly. The Catholic
accoutrements of the Temple and Lincoln's Inn
churches were the most resistant, with Lincoln's
Inn church retaining some deeply Catholic
features to this very day: hooded lawyers
processed with staves on festival days, and
stained glass windows decorated their chapels.

The communities around the Inn were
perfect for illicit Catholic dealings: isolated but
fairly wealthy communities surrounded by
marshes, woods and fields – close to both the
Thames and the Fleet in case escape was
needed, and outside the easy influence of both
London and Westminster. Out of a membership
of 180 lawyers at Middle Temple, an
investigation in 1578 revealed 80 suspected
Catholics, with lawyers like Edmund Plowden
and Matthew Smith openly refusing career
advancement in order to avoid taking the Oath
of Supremacy or allowing themselves to be

bound by regulations dictating church attendance and compulsory communion.

Yet lawyers continued to have a reputation for religious innovation: when John Swan writes of the dispossession of Mary Glover in 1603, he mentions that a young lawyer from the Middle Temple came to observe her fits. The exorcist John Darrel, as has been previously mentioned, was a former law student, leaving with a BA but never seeming to have practised. Marlowe's *Dr. Faustus* of 1592 had described Faust as, amongst other things, a lawyer, not unlike the real-world figure of Heinrich Cornelius Agrippa, who went from mercenary to cleric to lawyer to doctor to lawyer, poet, writer and back again, even trouncing the Wittenburg inquisition in an attempted land grab against an elderly woman accused of witchcraft.

These young lawyers, with access to London's vibrant book and manuscript trade (of which Shakespeare himself was an avid participant), would have had access to all the most lurid tales of the Darrel dispossessions, and the counterfeit case of Rachel Pinder in London. Candlemass would have been a good time for a play like *Twelfth Night*: Candlemass was a time of mixed mirth and foreboding, with the last remnants of the Christmas period being swept away on pain of death, and sailors refusing to set sail for fear of misfortune.

However, for one of the Templars present that night, Malvolio's troubles could have had a far more personal connotation.

Robert Brigges

One of the Templars present would certainly have been the respected and charitable Robert Brigges. Brigges had been a lawyer for some 20 years until 1599, when he had retired from practice, but continued to stand bond for young lawyers seeking entry to the Inns of Court. Brigges had never achieved high office, but seems to have invested shrewdly enough in business, and had done well enough to pay for the rebuilding of his chambers just before he retired.

However, at the age of 29, Brigges had been a demoniac. It had begun in 1573, after attending a Christmas lecture by a Lassier Villiers, where the preacher had argued against certain forms of sin and predestination. Brigges, unfortunately, had misunderstood the nature of the lecture, thinking that Villiers was arguing in favour of the very points that he was refuting.

The revelation that he was a predestined, damned and helpless sinner had driven Brigges into a terrible and deep depression. For months after the lecture, Brigges was openly suicidal:

"…[he] sought divers times meanes to destroy him selfe, sumtyme attempting to hang himself, sumtyme to cast himself downe headlong at his window, sumtyme running his hed against stone walls, divers tymes thrusting knives into himself, which, howe carefully soever his wife and shervantes hidd from him, where layed again in his way, nobody knows howe. Divers tymes he thought to drown himself in the Thames."[30]

The deeply depressed and despondent Brigges was troubled at all times by intrusive, impious thoughts, and it is very much worth noting his Puritan sensibilities in characterising his questioning, unfaithful and lustful thoughts as the external temptations of the Devil.

Eventually, Brigges decided to head over the river into Southwark. As many patrons of the Rose might have known, Southwark was a strange mix at the time: a red light district and an agricultural market; an industrial zone full of strangely bubbling chemicals surrounded by farms.

For whatever reason Brigges went to Southwark – the text of his possession says, "determining to make sure work at laste" – his metaphorical black dog quickly became a literal hound of hell. Stepping off a ferry boat onto the shores of the Bankside, the two handwritten accounts of the possession describe, "ther followed harde at his heales an uglye dogge, shagge heare, of a darke fuskey color, betweine blacke and red, wiche, when he prived to follow him weresoever he went, he strake at with his foote, and with stones, and also caused a digger of gravell in the field between Redrefe and Southworke to strike him with a sharpe spad with such force as might have cloven a dogg in the mydest. But all this never did him any harme, nether coulde drive hime awaye. Whereuppon the sayed Master Brigges withdrew himself to the Themes side, the dogge following him, he caste off his gowne, determining to have rune hedlonhe into the water. The dogge alye down upon the bancke and looked upon him with such terrible sparkling eyes that Master Brigges, beinge sore afrayed of him, thought with himself this no dowte is no dogge, but the devil...."[31]

Whatever the strange dog's nature, Brigges didn't drown himself and didn't stay in the water. He took refuge in a

'Black House' for a while (which, knowing the Bankside, could be anything from a theatre to a bar or a brothel, or even someone's private house) before getting on a boat back to London, and the black dog vanishing as quickly as it had appeared the moment he got on the ferry.

The incident with the dog, and Brigges' deep depression, were enough to persuade him to see a doctor, who recommended the contemporary treatments of blood letting and an 'ordinary poison', or 'potion', which Brigges continued to take for several days.

On April 11th, the medicine (which could have been anything from fairly harmless herbs to a cocktail of heavy metals) he seemed to have been taking for a few days caused Brigges to vomit and fall into a coma for several hours.

The next day, as his friends visited him, he fell into another fit, or trance, this time without the intervention of any medicine. Like Thomas Darling and the Starkie children, Brigges lost his senses, but for now seemed to keep control of his speech, prompting his friends to appoint a scribe so that they could write down the unusually interesting and erudite comments he seemed to be making about the Ten Commandments.

This is of note, particularly because although Brigges was obviously a religious man – a less religious man would hardly spend his Christmas attending a theological lecture – his scribes wrote that he was not a particularly learned man when it came to specific knowledge of scripture. Yet each day the religious-but-not-formally-knowledgeable Brigges was taken by a strange physical effect:

"His fitte frequented abowte 8th or 9th in the morning, take him every daye first with gaping and remynge lyke and ague, then darkness overspred his eyes by little and lytle, not without great angwishe and payne in his eye stringes and temples. Then wolde his herynge fale him, his felynge remanynge a food space after, but when the tempter came, hee presently loste his feeling also... differing nothing from a deed man but that he spake and drew breath."

It was also during this early time that his friends realised Brigges was part of a dialogue:

"...althowgh the sick man used many pawses lysteninge, as it seemed, to the voyce that spake unto him.... He would begyne to answer the tempter, aperinge unto him sumtyme in one hape and sumtyme in another."

As Brigges' pattern became established, he went public. Like Darling and the French demoniac Nicole Obry, his 'fits' attracted huge crowds:

"The tymes of his fittes where so well knowen to the howses of cowert as ther never failed bothe cownsalls at lawe and stundentes, sometimes a dossen, somtyme xxtie, and most tymes the chamber so full as none colde scarely stand by another, many time of which, for the better confirmation of the truthe, I have procured to subscribe their names to this booke."[32]

The result of this was that Brigges became a household name, and although Foxe was involved, Brigges was not

the same kind of demoniac as Webb and Pindar, or
Thomas Darling or Stephens. He was an empowered
demoniac who, although he did get help from Foxe,
eventually dispossessed himself and ran the course of his
visions. He lost his speech, he briefly lost his faith, after
being told that his friends were plotting against him and
meeting the beautiful Queen of Hell, but ultimately,
while Darling's narrative was subverted by the exorcist,
Brigges' ended with his victory: he hissed mockingly at
the devils of hell and defeated Satan in debate. His fits
lessened in severity until he returned to normal and
resumed his life as a lawyer.

The uniqueness of the narrative,
despite the distinctive features that avoided it
being a thing for both playwrights and
pamphleteers to cash in on, might well – must,
in fact – have been a story for the lawyers of
Middle Temple. "Why isn't Brigges a QC?"
"Oh lord, weren't you here…?" If that were the
case, even if Harsnett and Bancroft didn't see
Twelfth Night at the Whitehall on January 6th,
February 2nd would have certainly seen the high
jinks of Malvolio's possession resonate with the
lawyers assembled

Selected References

[1] TNA RYE/47

[2] A good example is in A Roger Ekirch, *At Day's Close: A
History of Nighttime*, Kindle Edition, Phoenix, 2013, loc. 794.
Here Ekirch tells us of a man who died after falling into a
London well. His neighbours did not rescue him for fear that he
was a demon.

[3] Kathleen R Sands, *An Elizabethan Lawyer's Possession by
the Devil: the Story of Robert Brigges*, Praeger, 2002, p. 96

[4] John Calvin & Henry Beveridge (tr), *Institutes of the Christian Religion*, Edinburgh Calvin Translation Society, p. 203

[5] Hugh Latimer & Rev. George Elwes Corrie (ed), *The Sermons of Hugh Latimer*, Cambridge University Press, 1844, p. 42. See also, Thomas Cranmer & William M Engles (ed), *Writings of Rev. Dr. Thomas Cranmer: Archbishop of Canterbury and Martyr, (1556)*, Presbyterian Board of Education, p. 215

[6] William Perkins, *A Discourse of the Damned Art of Witchcraft, So Farre forth as it is Revealed in the Scriptures, and Manifest by True Experience*, Cantrell Legge, 1618, p. 2

[7] These ideas are very well summarised in Nathan Johnstone, "The Protestant Devil: The Experience of Temptation in Early Modern England", *Journal of British Studies*, No. 43, April 2004, pp. 173–205

[8] Stephen Gosson, *The School of Abuse, Containing a Pleasant Invective Against Poets, Pipers, Players, Jesters, etc.*, The Shakespeare Society, 1841, pp. 27–28

[9] William Perkins, "The Combat Between Christ and the Devil Displayed", *The Works of That Most Famous and Worthy Minister of Christ in the University of Cambridge M W Perkins*, Vol. 3, 1631, p. 376

[10] George Gifford, *A discourse of the subtill practises of deuilles by witches and sorcerers...*, Toby Cooke, 1587, p. 28

[11] Augustine of Hippo & Rev. Marcus Dodds (ed), *The Works of Augustine, Bishop of Hippo*, T&T Clarke, 1876, Vol. 1, pp. 329–331

[12] Scott, p.ix

[13] James VI, King of Scotland, "Daemonologie in Forme of a Dialogue", Lawrence Normand & Gareth Roberts, *Witchcraft in Early Modern Scotland: James VI's Demonology and the North Berwick Witches*, University of Exeter Press, Digital Print Edition, 2011, p. 406

[14] A very good book on sermon exempla is Joan Young Gregg, *Devils, Women and Jews: Reflections on the Other in Medieval Sermon Stories*, SUNY, 1997. See also, David Jones, *Friars'*

Tales: Sermon Exempla from the British Isles, Manchester University Press, 2011. Individual author's works are also available, often for free, via websites like archive.org and Google Books.

[15] Nancy Caciola, "Wraiths, Revenants and Ritual in Medieval Culture", *Past and Present*, No. 152, Aug 1996, p. 14

[16] A very readable account of this can be found in Anne Somerset's *Unnatural Murder*, referenced above, and in Ian Donaldson, *Ben Jonson: A Life*, OUP, 2011. See also Beatrice White, *Cast of Ravens: The Strange Case of Sir Thomas Overbury*, George Braziller, 1965. Also, 'James 1 - volume 84: December 1615', in *Calendar of State Papers Domestic: James I, 1611-18*, HMSO, 1858, pp. 335–341; 'James 1 - volume 86: January 1616', in *Calendar of State Papers Domestic: James I, 1611-18*, HMSO, 1858, pp. 342–365; 'James 1 - volume 87: May 1616', in *Calendar of State Papers Domestic: James I, 1611-18*, HMSO, 1858, pp. 365–378; 'James 1 - volume 88: July 1616', in *Calendar of State Papers Domestic: James I, 1611-18*, 1858, pp. 378–392

[17] Philip Almond, "The Most Wonderful and True Story of a Certain Witch Named Alice Gooderige of Stapen Hill who was Arraigned and Convicted at Derby at the Assizes There", *Demonic Possession and Exorcism in Early Modern England: Contemporary Texts and Their Cultural Contexts*, Cambridge University Press, 2004, p. 158

[18] Samuel Harsnett, A *Discovery of the Fraudulent Practices of John Darrel...*, John Wolfe, 1599, p. 81

[19] Leslie Hotson, *The First Night of Twelfth Night*, Macmillan, 1954, p. 176

[20] Stephen Gosson, *Playes Confuted in Five Actions*, Thomas Gosson, 1582, n. pag

[21] Almond, "A Brief and True Discourse Containing the Certain Possession and Dispossession of Seven Persons in One Family in Lancashire...", 1600, p. 224

[22] Ibid, p. 19

[23] Almond, "A True and Fearful Vexation of One Alexander Nyndge...", p. 48; "A Brief Narration of the Possession,

Dispossession, and Repossession of William Sommers...", 1598, p. 248

[24] H von Scott & CC Bland (tr), *The Dialogue on Miracles: Caesarius of Heisterbach* (1220-1235), George Routledge and sons, 1929, p.15

[25] Almond, "A Brief and True Discourse Containing the Certain Possession and Dispossession of Seven Persons in One Family in Lancashire...", 1600, p. 210

[26] Almond, "A Brief Narration of the Possession, Dispossession, and Repossession of William Sommers...", 1598, p. 285

[27] Almond, "A Brief and True Discourse Containing the Certain Possession and Dispossession of Seven Persons in One Family in Lancashire...", 1600, p. 214

[28] Almond, "The Most Wonderful and True Story of a Certain Witch Named Alice Gooderige of Stapen Hill who was Arraigned and Convicted at Derby at the Assizes There", p. 159

[29] See Kathleen R Sands, *Demon Possession in Elizabethan England*, Praeger, Kindle Edition, 2004, n. pag; F W Brownlow, *Shakespeare, Harsnett and the Devils of Denham*, University of Delaware Press, 1993, which reproduces an excellent version of Harsnett's *A Declaration of Egregious Popish Impostures*.

[30] Sands, 2002, p. 96

[31] Ibid.

[32] Ibid, p. 98

Witches

JUSTICE: Here's none now, Mother Sawyer,
but this gentleman, myself and you:
let us to some mild questions;
have you mild answers;
tell us honestly and with a free confession –
we'll do our best to wean you from it
—are you a witch or no?
M. SAW: I am none.
JUSTICE: Be not so furious.
M. SAW: I am none. None but
base curs so bark at me;
I'm none: or would I were!
If every poor old woman be trod on thus by slaves,
reviled, kicked, beaten,
as I am daily,
she to be revenged
had need turn witch
-- Act 4, Scene 1, The Witch of Edmonton, William
Rowley, Thomas Dekker and John Ford, (1621)

While this chapter will touch upon what history likes to
call 'Cunning Women' – magico-medical practitioners
who really were performing acts that they believed were
magical, Mother Sawyer's speech in *The Witch of
Edmonton* exposes the reality of most women accused of
witchcraft in Early Modern England: poor and despised.

    The dissolution of the monasteries
created a welfare vacuum that wasn't righted
until the 1580s, and brought with it the simple
factor of job losses: when Butley Priory in
Suffolk was dissolved in 1538, 72 workers
became unemployed.[1] This came with a general

issue of high rents on land, and chronic underemployment. William Harrison, who contributed to *Holinshed's Chronicles*, wrote, "the daily oppression of the copyholders, whose lands seek to bring their poor tenants into plain servitude and usury. Doubling, tripling, and now and then seven times increasing their fines."[2]

The 1616 Sheffield census showed the plight of the small land owner: "not one of them can keep a team on his own land, and not above ten who have grounds of their own that will keep a cow." This would lead to a reliance on other forms of subsistence: wage work, which could be unreliable and low paying; gleaning (scavenging edible plants from common land) and begging. Particularly in small communities, those claiming alms from the parish would be known and visible. Some were loved – Joan Dan of Pluckley was buried by a fairly loving community, but seems to have alleviated their feelings of resentment by diligently maintaining part time work: something that might not have been available to other women.[3]

Another issue for the women who would become witches was the simple fact of their life expectancy, which could be far longer than a man's. While 16th and 17th century social mores were certainly oppressive, women were less likely to be at the places where men might contract diseases, or have lethal accidents. In turn, a long-lived woman could find herself either burying both her husband and sons, being left to bring up a child alone, or becoming the new wife of an established family and therefore the target of resentment.[4]

Compare this with a passage from the witchcraft sceptic Reginald Scott's book, *The Discoverie of Witchcraft:*

"These miserable wretches are so odious unto all their neighbours, and so feared, as few dare offend them or deny them anything they ask… These go from house to house and from door to door for a pot full of milk, yeast, drink, pottage, or some such relief, without the which they could hardly live… It falleth out many time that neither their necessities nor their expectation is answered or setved in those places where they beg or borrow, but rather their lewdness is by their neighbours reproved. And further, in tract of time the witch waxeth odious and tedious to her neighbours, and they again are despised and spited of her, so as sometimes she curseth one, and sometimes another, and from that the master of the house, his wife, children, cattle, etc. To the little pig that lieth in the stye. Thus in process of time they have all displeased her, and she hath wished evil luck unto all them, perhaps with curses and imprecations made in form. Doubtless at length some of her neighbours die or fall sick, or some of their children are visited with diseases that vex them strangely, as apoplexies, epilepsies, convulsions, hot fevers, worms, etc., which by more ignorant parents are supposed to be the vengeance of witches…"[5]

Finally, there is no better oration on the precarious life of an Early Modern woman than this later section of Act 4, Scene 1, from *The Witch of Edmonton*:

M. SAWYER: A witch! Who is not? Hold not that universal name in scorn, then. What are your painted things in princes' courts, upon whose eyelids lust sits, blowing fires to burn men's souls in sensual hot desires, upon whose naked paps a lecher's thought acts sin in fouler shapes than can be wrought?
JUSTICE: But those work not as you do.

*M. SAWYER: No, but far worse these by enchantments
can whole lordships change to trunks of rich attire, turn
ploughs and teams to Flanders mares and coaches, and
huge trains of servitors to a French butterfly. Have you
not city-witches who can turn their husband's wares,
whole standing shops of wares, to sumptuous tables,
gardens of stolen sin; in one year wasting what scarce
twenty win? Are these not witches?*

*JUSTICE: Yes, yes; but the law casts not an eye on
these.*

*M. SAWYER: Why, then, on my, or any lean old beldam?
Reverence once had wont to wait on age; now an old
woman, ill-favoured grown with years, if she be poor,
must be called bawd or witch. Such so abused are the
coarse witches; t'other are the fine, spun for the devil's
own wearing.*

*-- Act 4, Scene 1, The Witch of Edmonton, William
Rowley, Thomas Dekker and John Ford, (1621)*

Macbeth and the North Berwick Witch Trials: Enter the Sabbat

The witch's Sabbat, as described at length in the Berwick witch trials, comes to us first in the Alpine trials of 100–200 witches recorded by Johannes Frund (some counts go as high as 375, but in reality it's almost impossible to know how many witches were really burned).

In this trial, we get the first phantasmagorical account of the witches travelling to their Sabbat (or sometimes, Synagogue). Here we see them meet the Devil, where they recount their acts of black magic and worship him on their knees. How they get there is by the use of special ointments that allow them to fly through the air, either themselves or on prepared objects, made from the body of a newly killed child (which they sometimes eat).

Once the witches have been rewarded or rebuked by their master, they then dance wildly, sometimes degenerating into an orgy. This was one of the common accusations against heretics – they had weird sex, or had sex with the Devil, whose penis was commonly described (in great detail) as being either ice cold or burning hot, and who would finalise their obeisance with the 'foul kiss' – kissing the Devil on the arse.

Night-flying witches had been a 'thing' in popular imagination for some time: European folklore was full of bands of women – good and bad – who flew at night and either did good deeds, or came to people's houses and ate their food at night. Even the stories in the *Life of St. Germain*, referenced by a number of witchcraft writers in the Middle Ages and Early Modern period, contained a story where the divine caught a band of night-flying creatures who turned out to be demons in human form.

The idea of witches flying waned, and we can see the signs of its replacement in the North Berwick witch trials: John Fian's trial documents give us the vision of him flying with the Devil over the ocean, while Janet Stratton tells that Agnes Sampson took her soul out of her body to attend the Sabbat in spirit form only. This idea was even debated by Heinrich Kramer in his *Malleus Maleficarum*, where Kramer insisted that demons were helping women to travel to Sabbats by impersonating them in bed at night.

In fact, the idea of impersonation might be why Janet Stratton brought up her replacement, to cover for times where her confession put her in two places at once. This mental contortion was far from difficult for stunt thinkers like Kramer and the earlier Johannes Nider, both of whom stated that although there were women who *thought* they could fly at night, they weren't real witches.

The real witches were the ones who were really flying at night, and as Kramer suggested, getting demons to stand in for them in bed. Both Kramer and Nider suggested that when witches thought they saw people like the respectable English Ambassador Robert Bowes, they were being decieved shapechanging demons, who looked like innocent or important people so that they could fool witches into making false depositions.

History of Macbeth's Wyrd Sisters

In 1577, Raphael Holinshed published his *Holinshed's Chronicles*, the finished portion of a much more ambitious project to map the history of the world from the Biblical flood to the reign of Elizabeth I. This historical work was a huge influence on William Shakespeare, giving us the source material for plays like *Cymbeline*, *Macbeth* and *Henry V*.

    In *Holinshed*, we see much of the story of *Macbeth* told for us: the ambitious noble who lies and murders to become king and who is ousted by a man "never born of my mother, but ripped out of her wombe". Yet in *Holinshed's Chronicles* the three witches are described not as witches, but as "creatures of the Elder World", or Fairies.

It's certain that Shakespeare was aware of faeries. Certainly his audience would have been aware of them, not simply because of *A Midsummer Night's Dream*, but through Spencer's *Faerie Queene* and the role of the faerie in everyday English society. Cunning Women – local witches who offered medical services – still claimed their powers were due to faerie parentage, even as the rising Puritan sect painted them as demons taking forms that would deceive the weak minded.

    Even King James I expressed an opinion on faeries in his 1597 book *Daemonologie*, writing that numerous witches had gone to the stake (since the Scots burned witches) telling fantastical tales of being taken to faerie hills and being given magical stones with wondrous properties.

    Naturally, as a good Protestant, James insisted that faeries were nothing more than the delusions of the Devil, and that women who

said they travelled with the faeries, or any other
nocturnal court of good spirits, were being deceived by
the Devil.

Anglo-Saxon mythology shows a terrifying
female elf known as the Haegtesse, who rode across
burial mounds and liminal places associated with the
dead, and threw poisoned spears at people. Dr Alaric
Hall of Leeds University even shows the survival of the
Haegtesse into Early Modern culture by showing us the
trial of Isobel Gowdie, who was tried as a witch in 1662
at Nairn, mirroring the story of the Haegtesse by telling
of how she had ridden through the skies with her coven,
shooting elf-arrows at those below. We see the
transformation into something supernatural, and the idea
of transformation into something other than human in
Lady Macbeth's speech:

LADY MACBETH: The raven himself is hoarse
That croaks the fatal entrance of Duncan
Under my battlements. Come, you spirits
That tend on mortal thoughts, unsex me here,
And fill me from the crown to the toe top-full
Of direst cruelty. Make thick my blood.
Stop up the access and passage to remorse,
That no compunctious visitings of nature
Shake my fell purpose, nor keep peace between
The effect and it! Come to my woman's breasts,
And take my milk for gall, you murd'ring ministers,
Wherever in your sightless substances,
You wait on nature's mischief. Come, thick night,
And pall thee in the dunnest smoke of hell,
That my keen knife see not the wound it makes,
Nor heaven peep through the blanket of the dark
To cry "Hold, hold!"
-- Act 1, Scene 5, Macbeth, William Shakespeare, (1606)

Why then, did Shakespeare alter the narrative of his play from the Holinshed source material? We see in *A Midsummer Night's Dream* that he has no problem showing the faeries as a semi-antagonistic force (although it is strange that Oberon stresses his people's lack of fear when it comes to church bells, a traditional way to ward off demons).

The reason is that Shakespeare, like many other Londoners, was aware that the new King's life held a much more interesting story, waiting to be told. One that we see a glimpse of when the witches first appear:

THIRD WITCH: Sister, where thou?
FIRST WITCH: A sailor's wife had chestnuts in her lap, and munch'd and munch'd and munch'd – 'give me,' quoth I: 'Aroint thee, witch!' the rump-fed royon cries. Her husband's to Aleppo gon, master o' the Tiger: but in a sieve I'll thither sail, and like a rat without a tail, I'll do, I'll do, and I'll do.
SECOND WITCH: I'll give thee a wind.
FIRST WITCH: Thou'rt kind.
THIRD WITCH: And I another.
FIRST WITCH: And I myself have all the other, and the very ports they blow, all the quarters that they know, I' the shipman's card, I will drain him dry as hay: sleep shall neither night nor day hang upon his pent-house lid; He shall live a man forbid: weary se'n nights nine times nine shall he dwindle, peak and pine: though his bark cannot be lost, yet it shall be tempest-tost.
Look what I have.
SECOND WITCH: Show me, show me.
FIRST WITCH: Here I have a pilot's thumb, wreck'd homeward he did come.
-- Act 1, Scene 3, Macbeth, William Shakespeare, (1606)

The Childhood of King James I, His Marriage, and the Battle for a Nation

James became king at thirteen months old, and spent his childhood in the custody of various powerful men vying for regency. His childhood had been characterised by repeated kidnap and manipulation by a series of powerful men, ending with James breaking free and emancipating himself after the Ruthven Raid, and the passing of the 1584–85 'Black Acts' reaffirming the powers of the bishops and driving a number of Presbyterian ministers to exile in England.

By 1587, the King was 21 and his marriage was a pressing concern. He had been attracted to his cousin, Esme Stuart, when he had been thirteen years old, but by 1587 his councillors demanded a marriage.

King James chose a Danish princess because of the trading links between Scotland and Denmark. The marriage was delayed only when it was uncovered that his Captain of the Guard – the Earl of Huntly – had sent letters of support for the Spanish Armada of 1588, and had staged a rebellion when challenged. The Earl of Bothwell, James' cousin and detractor, had marched with Huntly, ending their rebellion when faced down by the King and his forces at the Brig of Dee, outside Aberdeen. By June 1589, James had successfully proposed his marriage to his second choice bride, Anne, after negotiations for the hand of her older sister Elizabeth had come to nothing. Denmark renounced its claim to the Orkney and Shetland Isles, and Anne was to be given the Lordship of Falkland, with Dunfirmline as James' personal gift.

As the Danish Royal Family began lavish preparations for the wedding, James' Scotland wallowed in deprivation: famine and bad financial management had left the country in abject poverty. James had only broken the apron strings and taken control over his country in 1583, and although he was to prove a good financial manager, the same couldn't be said for his regents. By contrast, the Danish could afford to make a carriage entirely out of silver.

By August 1589, the Earl Marischal had stood in for James at a ceremonial wedding in Copenhagen. Anne was due to sail out to Scotland, landing at Leith, where James waited in the house of Robert, 6th Lord Seton, where he could see the Firth of Forth and be ready to preside over the ceremonies planned for Anne's arrival.

When Anne hadn't arrived by early October, the King's mixture of worry and embarrassment was palpable. The courtier Sir James Melville describes the King's demeanour after having heard the news of her delay:

"…his Maieste remainit quietly in the castell of Craigmyllair, not content with the maist part of his consaill, as said is, and culd not sleip nor rest… in the mean tym, he directed the crownell Stuart to my brother Sir Robert and me, charging us to tak cair of his mishandled estate in tym commyng; laanting how that he was abused by sic as he had over mekle reposed upon, and that he had always found us faithful and cairfull for his wealfairel; willing us to sit down and advyse how he mycht best remedy to thingis past, and eschew six inconvenientis in tymes commyng…"[6]

By October 8th, a series of alarming, telegram-like notes had been exchanged between the Scottish Ambassador in London and the King's agents in Denmark: "Expectation of the Princess of Denmark; contrary winds; the King's trouble; surmises; Col. Stewart sent to search for the fleet; non-arrival of the princess; fear of disaster; omens; public fast and prayer; Col. Stewart not returned."

The Princess and her entourage had sailed on the flagship, The Gideon, on September 1st, but a leak had forced them to take shelter in Norway, where a violent storm had thwarted their attempts to sail. By the end of September, the fleet had attempted to sail again but The Gideon had immediately sprung a leak, forcing her back into port. Col. Stewart had arrived, concurring with Earl Marischal that the effort should be abandoned and the party return to Denmark overland.

    Accidents due to storms were also striking at home, and in most embarrassing ways: Sir James Melville's sister-in-law, Jean Kennedy, had set sail from Burntisland to Leith when her vessel had been sunk in a storm. Jean had been chosen as one of Anne's gentlewomen and the loss of both her and the boat would have been a great embarrassment. Her brother-in-law's reaction mentions explicitly that witches were involved, saying that they had confessed to His Majesty that they had done the deed:

"The stormes wer also sag ret heir, that ane boit perissit between Bruntsland and Leith, wherin was a gentilwoman callit Jene Kenete, wha had bene lang in England with the Quen his Maiesties mothe and was sen syn married upon my brother the maiser houshald to hir Maiestie, Sir Andro Melville of Garuok. Quhilk gentilwoman being descret and grave, was sent for be his Maieste, to be about the Quen his bedfallow. Sche being willing to mak deligence, wald not stay, for the storm, to sail the ferry; wher the vehement storm drave a schip forceably upon the said boit, and drownit the gentilwoman and all the personnes exept twa. This the

Scotis witches confessit unto his Maiestie to have
done."[7]

At the same time, the Kirk was busily trying to establish
itself as a sovereign authority, reporting directly to the
King, rather than accepting the King's role as God's
mediator on Earth. From 1574 until the 1580s, the
Presbyterian wish to establish a full Presbyterian system
in Scotland created a struggle between the Church and
State, with Andrew Melville and twenty other ministers
who would later participate in the witch hunts, going into
a temporary exile in England over James' Black Acts.
        Within this period of tension, witches
were a crucial force in cementing the cracks
between James and the Kirk. From 1587,
Maitland, the Scottish chancellor, had brought a
spirit of greater cooperation between the Kirk
and State, along with the exiled ministers
returning from London, where one of them,
James Carmichael, was appointed "a judge of
ecclesiastical causes". During Carmichael's
exile after the Black Acts, he had made some
contacts in the world of London printing –
contacts that would possibly become important.
As a staunch Presbyterian, he took power with
all the expected attitudes, stating that his
explicit aim in Scotland was that "Sathan,
Antichrist and his supporters may be quite
houndit out of ther nests."
        Returning to the King's troubles with
his bride, by 1590 James decided to take
matters fully into his own hands. He went
personally to Denmark to marry his Queen in
person and bring her home to Scotland. The
return trip, starting on April 26th 1590, was
another troubled, stormy voyage, and just after

the royal couple returned to Scotland on May 1st the following year, six witches were tried and executed in Denmark for casting magical spells against the royal couple.

Witches in the Lives of the Powerful

It is worth a momentary aside. While many of the
confessions in the history of the North Berwick trials
were the results of torture and an active imagination,
Early Modern audiences would certainly not have been
shocked by the idea that the rich and powerful amongst
them were enlisting the help of witches:

HECATE: What death is't you desire for Almachildes?
DUCHESS: A sudden and a subtle.
HECATE: Then I have fitted you. Here lie the gifts of
both sudden and subtle: His picture made in wax and
gently molten by a blue fire kindled with dead men's eyes
will waste him by degrees.
DUCHESS: In what time, prithee?
HECATE: Perhaps in a moon's progress.
DUCHESS: What? A month? Out upon pictures, if they
be so tedious! Give me things with some life.
HECATE: Then seek no farther.
DUCHESS: This must be done with speed, dispatch'd
this night, if it may possible.
HECATE: I have it for you. Here's that will do't: stay
but perfection's time, and that's not five hours hence.
-- Act 5, Scene 2, The Witch, by Thomas Middleton,
(1613–16)

Even London's middle classes were depicted as resorting
to magic when all else failed:

CUDDY BANKS: I would I might else! But, witch or no
you are a motherly woman; and though my father be a
kind of the God-Bless-Us, as they saym U have an
earnest suit for you; and if you'll be so kind to ka me one
good turn, I'll be so courteous to kob you another.

*MOTHER SAWYER: What's that? To spurn me, beat me,
and call me witch, as your kind father doth?*
*CUDDY BANKS: My father! I am ashamed to own him.
If he has hurt the head of thy credit, there's money to buy
thee a plaster [gives her money]; and a small courtesy I
would require at your hands.*
*MOTHER SAWYER: You seem a good young man, and –
[Aside] I must dissemble, the better to accomplish my
revenge – but, for this silver, what wouldst have me do?
Bewitch thee?*
*CUDDY BANKS: No, by no means; I am bewitched
already: I would have thee so good as to unwitch me, or
to witch another with me for company.*
*MOTHER SAWYER: I understand thee not, be plain my
son.*
*CUDDY BANKS: As a pike-staff, mother. You know Kate
Carter?*
*-- Act 2, Scene 1, The Witch of Edmonton, by William
Rowley, Thomas Dekker and John Ford, (1621)*

Neither of these stories were without counterpart in the
everyday lives of English and Scottish citizens. Not only
the Carrs fell foul of using poison and for advancement.
It was something James had experience of in his youth.
In the direct aftermath of James' battle with his
rebellious dukes just outside Aberdeen, he had visited
the city in order to meet the witch Marion MacIngaroch,
the guest of Hector Munro, kinsman of Katherine Ross –
all of whom would find themselves on trial for
witchcraft.

     In Lady Katherine's case, the events had taken
place in 1577, decades before the young King's visit,
when Katherine had been possessed of a desire to prune
the family tree. If her accusers are to be believed, she
had decided to remove her son Robert Munro, and the
wife of her son George, so that when Robert died,

George would be free to marry his widow.
These attempted murders, first by magic and
then by poison, would see her next eldest son
Hector ascend to the title of Baron of Foulis,
while George would marry the otherwise
inconvenient widow (it is, of course, possible
that she was potentially quite willing – being a
young woman herself, and George being a
younger man).

Whether or not the acts depicted in
Lady Foulis' indictment, or 'dittay,' ever really
happened, the documents echo motifs redolent
in the interrogations and accusations of the
North Berwick witches:

"…in company with Cristian Roiss Malcome sone, and
vheris eftir specefeit… thow art accusit, for the making
of twa pictouris of clay, in cumpany with the said
Cristaine Roiss wethir chalmer in Canorth; the ane, maid
for the distructiounne and consumptioune of the young
Laird of Fowlis, and vther for the young Ladie
Balnagoune; to the effect that ane theirof ould be putt att
the Brig-end of Fowles, and the vther at Ardmoir, for
distructioun of the saidis young Laird and Lady: and this
should be performed at Alhallowmes in the year of God
1577: quhilkis twa pictouris, being sett on the sorth side
of the chalmer, the said Loskie Loncart tuik twa elf
arrow heides and deyuerit ane to ye Katherene, and the
vther, the said Cristian Rois Malcumsone held in her
awin hand; and thow schott twa schottis wit hthe said
arrow heid, att the said Lady Balnagowne, and Laskie
Loncart schott thrie schottis at the said young Laird of
Foulis: in the meane tyme, baith the pictouris brak and
thow commandit Laskie Loncart to make of new vthir
twa pictouris thaireftir…"

Katherine did not content herself with shooting flint arrows at the 'pictouris', or clay dolls. She ordered her compatriots to procure poison, which she had made into a drink and sent to her victims, which caused both to be grievously ill. The twenty-eighth item on her dittay even depicts her losing her temper – very reminiscent of a late trial depiction of the Earl of Bothwell – and throwing the 'pictouris' into the fire so that they would be destroyed quickly.[8]

In Katherine's case, her trial documents reveal her pursuer was her own son, Hector. A while before their audience with the King, the two had quarrelled, with Katherine making a complaint that Hector had been trying to dispossess her of her lands in Foulis by intimidating her tenants and using a commission against "witchecraft and utheris fogeit and feinyeit crymes…" to persecute them.

Hector, however, was far from blameless. Oddly, his dealings with magic had involved an act of relative benevolence: in 1588, some years after the events of his mother's trial, Hector had assembled a small group of male and female magical practitioners to attempt a cure of his brother Robert, who had fallen ill. The group had started using a lock of hair and some nail parings to cure the ailing baron, but had ultimately aborted their effort out of fear of Hector's father, who was working under a commission to investigate deaths by poisoning and witchcraft.

Sickness and its cure seem to have been the central reason for Hector's dealings with the occult. The second item on his dittay is that earlier that year, in January, he had sent a friend to seek the witch Marion MacIngaroch. At this time, Hector was ill – we can presume, gravely – and sought her advice on how to be cured:

"ye socht responsis att hir, and travellit to be curit be hir deviliseh Incataciounes and Wichecraft: Lyke asm sche, eftir lang consultacioun had with hir, sche declarit tht their wes na remeid for yow… to recover your health, without the principall man of your blue sould suffer death for yow; and ye and your complices haifing raknit with your selffis, quha this sould be, ffand that it wes George Monro, eldest sone to Katherene Roisse Lady Fowles."

Having decided that in order for him to live, George – for whom Lady Katherine had been scheming to secure a young wife – had to die. He was invited to attend his brother's bedside. Marion coached Hector in a magical technique that involved clasping his brother's right hand in his left and not speaking to him. Eventually, when all was prepared and George had visited Hector's sick bed enough times, Hector was placed in a symbolic grave, whereafter he stood in George's shoes, and was put back to bed with the further injunction not to speak.
The spell seems to have worked. In the trial dittay, stating that James had examined a pair of magical stones that Marion had attempted to use to cure Hector before the fatal spell on George, we are told:

"…quhair scho being exminat before his Maiestie, and produceit the stainis sche gaif yow watter out of, the quhilk wes the deith of the said George…"[9]

Hector seems to have been grateful to Marion. After his illness, the dittay states that he took her to his father and brother's house, where she was treated as if she was his wife, and given the token job of caring for his sheep – perhaps to bring an air of respectability to the scandal of a relationship between a nobleman and a Cunning Woman. It would certainly not have been the first time:

the extensive diaries of Goodwin Wharton show that a relationship founded in magical consultation – in this case, with Mary Parish, a magical practitioner considerably older than him – could end in marriage.

Even after the fall of Robert and Frances Carr in 1613, powerful families using magicians to settle their affairs would remain in the public consciousness. In 1620, one John Chamberlain wrote to Dudley Carleton, the Viscount Dorchester:

"…one Peacocke, sometimes a schoolmaster and a minister (but a very busie-brained fellow) was last weeke committed to the Tower for practising to infatuate the King's judgement by sorcerie (they say) in the business of Sir Thomas Locke and the Lady of Exeter, he hath ben strictly examined by the Lord Chancellor, the Lord Cooke, the Lord Chief Justice, and Attorney Solicitor and others, and on Tuesday was hanged up by the wrists, though he were very impatient of the torture and swooned once or twice, yet I cannot learne that they have wrought any greate matter out from him: Sir Thomas Locke was confronted with him at the Lord Chancellor's, where upon [text becomes illegible]."[10]
While we cannot know what courtly gossip made of him, when William Camden wrote of Peacock in his diary, he was scathing:;']21

"Peacock of Cambridge, who had claimed he had employed magical tricks to sway the King's mind away from sound judgement in the case of Thomas Locke, is put to torture in the Tower of London. Some pronounced him a madman, others an imposter."[11]

Certainly Peacock seems to have been treated with relative leniency compared to other magicians who had attempted to influence the King. Two years later there was a letter from the Lord Lieutenant of the Tower ordering that Peacock be taken from there to the much lower priority (and less well appointed) Marshalsea Prison, where he vanishes from the historical record.

Enter the Witches

Returning to North Berwick, the fires of the witch trials were beginning to smoulder in Scotland.

In September of 1589, Agnes Sampson, a midwife and generally benevolent mystic of a type known as a 'Cunning Woman', was charged with witchcraft, for which she was investigated and tried by the authorities at Haddington. She was a fairly benevolent practitioner: using folk remedies such as herbs and vinegar to heal members of the local community. She was also a magical practitioner: if it is not a fabrication of her interrogators, Agnes admitted that she had used a magical prayer on the Lady Kilbarberton. In the document accompanying her interrogation she describes how the prayer was able to tell her whether a patient would improve or decline; how she could use it as a magical spell to heal them; and to aid the work of natural remedies.

If this is true, Sampson was one of the few witches tried whose magic wasn't a fabrication. She could have long practised healing and divination. Her personal religion, although not developed in any deliberate doctrine, was deeply Catholic, including a belief in the spiritual power of the saints. The original reason for her being charged isn't clear, but during her interrogation, probably confused and under pressure to make a confession that pleased her jailers, the unfortunate midwife made mention of some current events. Even in her earliest interrogations, Sampson had been pressed on whether she had used magic to harm the King and his allies.

Her first session with the interrogators of Haddington Tollbooth seems to have taken place over a long period, with her 'interviews' divided over at least two sessions. On a Saturday morning, some time before

December 1590, she mentioned the king
directly for the first time:

> "She confesses that the devil said it should be
> hard to the king to come home and that the
> queen should never come home except the
> king fetched her. She enquired whether the
> king would have lads or lasses. He answered
> that he should have lads then lasses."[12]

Sampson and another woman – Gellis Duncan, about
whom little is known – both confessed to repeated
meetings of witches, and to being visited in prison by the
Devil, who arrived in a fire that swept from the top of the
prison to the bottom. Duncan even confessed that their
group of witches received a letter stating that they should
raise a storm to prevent the Queen's coming to Scotland.

Sampson's confession was sufficiently
interesting to attract James' personal attention.
In a session with him, Sampson confessed to the
typical trappings of witchcraft as constructed by
Continental witchcraft writers like Heinrich
Kramer and Johannes Nider: that she was
commanded by the Devil to renounce Christ;
that she made a pact upon promises of wealth
and food, and that she was physically marked
by the Devil upon taking up his service.

The two women also named a host of
accomplices, saying that they had met on a
bridge near the land belonging to the King's
friend, David Seton, and thrown a knotted rope
over the side, pulling the Devil up from the
river like a huge fish:

"She confesses that the goodwife of Spilmerford, 'Grey
Meal', Gellis Duncan, Bessie Thomson, Janet Stratton,
and herself with certain others, to the number of nine
convened at Foulstruther, and there had their

consultation how they might wrack David Seton and his goods.

"And first Gellis Duncan, Bessie Thomson, and 'Grey Meal' hauled a cord at the bridge and she cried 'Haul! Hola!' The end of it was very heavy […] had drawn the devil came up at the end of it and speered them all..."[13]

They also confessed to cursing Seton's cattle, although in later confessions this changed to admitting that they had attempted to curse Seton himself, but had unfortunately only succeeded in sickening his daughter.

Sampson and Duncan also confessed that they had pulled the Devil up on a rope in another place, and that also she met her fellow witches on a boat where they drank wine, and danced a wild Sabbat in the cemetery of the North Berwick Kirk before convening inside for a Satanic sermon.

By January 1591, Sampson was questioned by the King's Master of Work, an official at the heart of James' administration, but certainly not a professional judge or investigator. Here, she implicated the second of our three great witches: Barbara Napier. While Agnes Sampson was a respected commoner, Napier was related to Scottish nobility: her husband was Archibald Douglass, brother of the Laird of Carschogill.

Barbara was certainly a gentlewoman, if not nobility herself. Sampson's last confession (the document is dated a few days before her execution on January 28th 1591) described how she was consulted by Napier, who sent her maid to make an appointment where she could ask for Napier's assistance in first killing her husband, and in enchanting a ring so that she could gain the favour of a Lady Angus. This is fairly credible: during the life of James' cousin Henry, a young nobleman had gotten into trouble for plotting his father's

death with a magician who had originally
promised him a magical ring.

It was now that the rest of the witches
came into play: three men – John Fian, Donald
Robson and Richie Graham – were brought in,
along with Bessie Thompson and Janet Stratton.
Together they accused Napier and another
wealthy gentlewoman called Euphame
MacCalzean. In a description that might well
have been familiar from the trial of Lady
Katherine, the captured witches described the
use of a wax doll or 'picture':

"Donald Robson… confesses there were more nor
twenty at the convention at Acheson's Haven that
handled the picture. Agnes Sampson brought the picture
[wax doll] to the field; she delivered it to Barbara
Napier. Fra Barbara it was given to Euphame
MacCalzean; fra Euphame to Meg Begtoun of
Spilmersford. It passed through eight or nine more
women. At last it came to Robin Grierson; fra him to the
devil. They spake all 'James the Sixth' amongst them
handling the picture. The devil was like a man..."[14]

Bothwell is Implicated

It is not fully clear who first implicated Francis Stewart, Earl of Bothwell. A letter exists suggesting that it might have been the necromancer Richie Graham, who wrote a letter to the King and received some brief reward for denouncing the Earl as his client in black magic. Certainly, in the interrogations of the North Berwick witches, Donald Robson's is the first deposition to specifically name the Earl of Bothwell:

"Agnes Sampson said that there would be both gold and silver and victual gotten fra my Lord Bothwell. There were… Charles Wat in Garvet, who offered to deliver the picture back to the thief again to cummer the king."[15]

When Gellis Duncan was reinterrogated, she said that a "little black and fat man with black hair… soone after the king's departure into Denmark… had been with them in a cellar and given them gold to hange up and charm a toad for the hurte of the king in his life, and to hunder the isue to come of his bodie…"[16]

      Certainly, this was believed to have been the English ambassador, Robert Bowes. In a letter to Lord Walsingham, Bowes himself complained that one of the witches had accused him, but seemed not to have taken the allegation seriously. When Janet Stratton was reinterrogated the day after Agnes Sampson's death, she also implicated the ambassador, saying that she had heard him speaking to Euphame MacCalzean and Barbara Napier in a cellar or back room in Edinburgh, where a letter was opened from the Earl of Bothwell.

      When Stratton was examined by the King's own agents – particularly Bothwell's enemy, the King's chancellor – she painted a picture of a dire magical

ceremony taking place at the 'fiery hills of
Prestonpans' the previous Lammas Eve:

"In this matter was no other thing done while about a
month or thereby before the meeting at the Fiery Hills of
Prestonpans which was upon Lammas Eve that last was.
Anne Sampson got the toad and dripped the same above
the fire in her house, and after she had gotten the same
dripping in a latten dish, she caused this deponer get the
mixture or wash for her part, who brought the same to
Anne Sampson's house, where the same was mixed
together and heated on the fire, Anne Sampson stirring
the same with her three finger...

"...the dripping of the toad mixed, as said is, was also
black as pitch and was sent to Edinurgh to the women
who should use it there. At the mixing of it Anne
Sampson incalled the enemy saying 'My Master' three
times...

"...The purpose of their convening at that time was to
conjure or enchant a picture of wax which Anne
Sampson brought with her and showed to them that were
with her by the gate... Anne Sampson having the said
picture first in her left hand which she, at the devil's
bidding delivered to Barbara Napier... [and] Anne
Sampson said to the devil 'Take there the picture of
James Stewart, Prince of Scotland. And I ask of you,
Master Mahoun that I may have this turn wrought and
done, to wrack him for my Lord Bothwell's sake and for
the gold and silver that he has promised and should give
us, with victual to me and my bairns."[17]

As the trials of the witches neared, the confessions
strayed further and further from reality – Bothwell is
described as being at a Sabbat and enraging Sampson by

trying to snatch the wax doll and throw it straight onto the fire.

Witches described themselves dancing, feasting and kissing the Devil's arse at the Sabbat in the North Berwick Kirk. The unfortunate John Fian (a chancer and schoolteacher from Prestonpans) gave a straight-out-of-the-book account of flying with the Devil, skimming over the surface of the water until he reached a boat where he joined other witches and acted as the Devil's clerk during their Sabbat.

Fian also reiterates the transgressive deeds the witches took part in: the dismemberment of children and the disjointing of corpses at the North Berwick churchyard, where he describes witches with clasp knives running to and fro so that they could break open graves and take pieces of the bodies within.

Predictably, the witches were all dead by the summer of 1591. Bothwell fared slightly better, escaping imprisonment at Edinburgh Castle in 1591 and managing to stay at liberty until returning to kidnap the King in 1592. Although Bothwell is the one member of the group who was successfully found innocent of witchcraft (Napier's defenders initially succeeded in having her acquitted, until the King stepped in to threaten the jury with imprisonment themselves), sadly his success wasn't to last.

The King worked to undermine Bothwell's success – the Earl had been a successful and charismatic alternative to James, even going as far as to question James' legitimacy, but after the Stuart monarch successfully reconciled with Bothwell's Catholic allies in the North of Scotland, his strength faltered. Even when Bothwell was briefly sponsored by Queen Elizabeth, who used him as a bargaining tool against James to force the Stuart monarch to crush the northern Catholics, his strength did not recover. By 1595,

Bothwell's power was gone and his Catholic allies had fled into a voluntary exile. History records that he died in Naples.

News From Scotland

It's certain, since we have some of Robert Bowes' letters to the Queen's intelligencer William Cecil (Lord Burghley) summarising developments in the whole affair, that the gossip mills of London were alive with whispers of the King's problems and the issue of the Scottish witches. James himself would write his own book about the war against Satan and the supernatural – entitled *Daemonologie*– in 1594, but the trials were popularised by a pamphlet that would have come to England in the winter of 1591–92. In fact, it's likely that the pamphlet was written at royal behest to put a controlled spin on whatever rumours were already circulating in England and Scotland.

The author is officially unknown, but could have been James Carmichael, the minister of Haddington, where the whole affair started, and who was named as a possible author in the memoirs of Sir James Melville, who you will remember took part in interrogations.

Carmichael was connected with English publishing from his time in exile, where he'd been employed in various literary activities in London's Cheapside area. He was even acquainted with key figures like the English ambassador Robert Bowes and the unfortunate Earl of Angus, whose death (and the wife of whom) would appear in Barbara Napier's trial documents.

In the pamphlet, which comes to little more than fifteen pages of A4 when transcribed, we hear interesting details (although they may be fabricated).

Gellis Duncan's story begins with her being questioned by David Seton because she had started to vanish from her position as a servant during the night, and had suddenly started to practise healing skills.

Under interrogation (and physical tortures that included thumbscrews, having her head crushed with rope, and having her fingernails torn out with pliers) Duncan admitted that she had been involved with witchcraft. She named some familiar figures: Barbara Napier, Euphame MacCalzean, John Fian. (Interestingly, despite the real trial being very evenly gendered, *News from Scotland* concentrates on Fian, although Robert Grierson is mentioned).

Here James is described as witch hunter extraordinaire: the power of witches is nothing against his legitimate Kingship and he interrogates them all until finding the Devil's mark on them and squeezing out their true stories.

Here, Agnes Sampson is described as a great witch and the confidant of the Devil. It's also made clear in *News* (although the idea is present in the various trial documents) that the witches were also responsible for the death of Sir James Melville's sister-in-law, as well as causing the problems with both Anne's initial attempts to reach Scotland, and the King's return from Copenhagen.

John Fian is elevated to a huge role in the affair, which is strange, since his role in the trial documents is minimal: there is no record of his interrogation before his trial, and what he contributes is colour more than anything else. It's possible that he only got such a prominent role because of the timing; after all, Johannes Spiess' *Faustbook* came to England in 1591–92.

Fian's story gets more pages than any of the other individual witches: he is tortured by Seton, who breaks his legs with 'the boots' and crushes his skull by winding and tightening a rope, and his adventures as a magician (including a magical misadventure straight out of Apauleius' *The Golden Ass*).

The important thing, though, is that between James' *Daemonologie* and *News From Scotland*, the idea of the Scottish witch interfering in politics would have been strongly associated with England's Scottish King.[18]

To modern people, there is no great thing in seeing the three witches on a blasted heath in the middle of nowhere. We see three women who summon the terrible spirit of Hecate, but for the Jacobean audience these women would have been connected with an incalculably huge and sinister 'anti-religion' of Satanic witches.

An Anti-Religion

The idea of an anti-religion was nothing new. Medieval Christians had persecuted Jews, lepers and Muslims during the 14th century. Things went as far as to engage in mass executions of Jews and lepers during the 1320s in the South of France, in an episode known as "The Lepers' Plot", where lepers in the pay of Jews (who were in the pay of Muslim princes) had poisoned the wells and rivers of the South of France and northern Spain.

In Germany during the Black Death, flagellants and other bigots had accused Jews of spreading the plague, again fostering the idea that they abused the host and melted down the corpses of dead and kidnapped babies to make poisonous fats and powders that they could use to spread the 'plague', which was actually the Jews poisoning people.

Over time, the same libel was applied repeatedly to other groups: the Templars were accused of consorting with Satan and performing transgressive rituals. Part of the root of this was political necessity: as the outward enemies of Christianity dropped away, so new enemies needed to be found, but there was more.

From the *Book of Revelation* onwards, Christianity had always had an apocalyptic slant. Through the Middle Ages, Christian thinkers wrestled with it: Augustine pronounced that the Apocalypse wasn't tied to the fortunes of any one nation, but that there would be a series of cosmic days, known as Etates, that spaced out the phases of creation. Joachim of Fiore and other apocalyptic thinkers wrangled over the length of the Etates and which one we were in.

Unfortunately, as the year 1000 rolled in, theologians agreed that it was the year of the Apocalypse. Even when the world spun on, they agreed that since the Etates were longer than a single day, so the Apocalypse would be longer than they'd previously thought – they now lived in a world where Satan was free from hell, and was building his army for the final fight against God at the end of days.

This language was employed in entirely orthodox debates: John Bale, the Protestant writer, using the language of Apocalypse against Catholicism, said that it was the Devil's perversion of the Christian Church in preparation for the end of the world.

The language of the Apocalypse had begun to be used against witches during the 15th century. In the Dominican inquisitor Johannes Nider's book, *Formicarius*, he talks about gatherings of witches in the French Duchy of Lausanne where a demon would visibly appear and the witches would promise transgressions against the Christian faith, like trampling the Eucharist and spitting on the cross.

When, amongst the anti-heretic crusades rooting out Cathars and Waldenesians, thinkers like Jean Veneti and Nicholas Jacquier began arguing that witches were a new heretical sect, an army of Satan.

The Disempowerment of Witches

One significant difference between the scholarly magic of *Doctor Faustus* and the phantasmagoric, fantastical magic of *Macbeth* is the emphasis not only on transgressive ingredients, but also on external forces for their power to bewitch. In Johannes Nider's *Formicarius*, he writes, "The broom that the witch immerses in the water, so that it should rain, does not cause the rain, but a demon sees this... the witch gives a sign with the broom but the demon acts, so that it rains through the action of the demon."[19]

James I, in *Daemonologie*, wrote "The witches ar servantes onlie, and slaves to the Devil; but the Necromanciers his maisters and commanders."

This is part of a hugely important step in understanding the role of the witch in the mind-set of Shakespeare's audiences: while witches were dangerous to society – we see their power in *Macbeth* – the label of witch was critical in disempowering the accused, rather than giving them greater powers. The popular image of the male magician is the one we see in *Doctor Faustus* and *The Merry Devil of Edmonton*'s Peter Fabell: doomed, but nevertheless brilliant.

The witch is a different figure. In the trial of Elizabeth Sawyer from 1566, the inspiration for Rowley, Dekker and Ford's play, she is captured, fairly brutally, by the Devil: swearing on her way home:

"The first time that the Divell came unto me was, when I was cursing, swearing and blaspheming; he then rushed in upon me, and never before that time did I see him, or he me: and when he, namely the Divel, came to me, the first words that he spake unto me were there: *Oh! have I now found you cursing, swearing, and blaspheming? now you are mine.*

"He asked of me, when hee came unto me, how I did and what he should do for me, and demanded of mee my soule and body; threatening then to teare me in peeces, if that I did not grant unto him my soule and my body which he asked of me."[20]

Witch-hunting manuals certainly set their sights on women as being weak and porous to sin. In the *Cannon Episcopi*, as collected by Gratian in his *Corpus Iuris Canonici*, we read of, "certain accursed women 'been turned right back to Satan' and led astray... If only these women had been the only ones to die in their treachery and had not dragged many other people with them into the violent and untimely death of faithlessness!... There is no doubt that Satan himself, who transforms himself into an angel of light, captures the mind of some silly little woman... by using her lack of faith and lack of belief... then dupes her mind..."[21]

While many witches were poor – the majority of witchcraft narratives begin with a witch begging for some sort of charity and being refused – the disempowerment and scapegoating effect of being accused as a witch was a good way to silence uppity women. Both North Berwick defendants Barbara Napier and Euphame MacCalzean had money of their own – Napier from the death of her father and husband, and MacCalzean from being the heiress of Lord Cliftonhall, and is described as having, 'lands, heritages, tacks, steadings, rooms, possessions, corns, cattle, goods and gear'. MacCalzean also wields a power over men that is not often heard of in Early Modern women. Although her husband is referred to as 'Patrick Moscrop' in all trial documents during the North Berwick witch hunt, Yeoman, in the *Oxford Dictionary of National Biography*, writes that Mosscrop – MacCalzean's second husband – agreed to adopt the surname MacCalzean upon their marriage of 1570.[22] This is possibly due to the fact of MacCalzean's considerable fortune: although born illegitimate, she was recognised by her father before his death and inherited assets worth £3000.

Napier was the daughter of a family of Edinburgh burgesses – freemen and members of the ruling body of the city of Edinburgh – who might well have represented the city's interests to Parliament. Napier's first husband was a bookseller and her second was the brother of the Laird of Corshogill. Napier herself had been a lady in service to the Countess of Angus.

An important note on these final witches is that both are accused by those closest to them. MacCalzean was accused of attempting to kill her husband Patrick by either magic or poison, and was represented in the trial as a scandalously disobedient wife: she was portrayed as such a terrible shrew that her husband fled abroad soon after their marriage, and was only able to secure his love by using love potions and other forms of magic. She was also accused of murdering her husband's nephew, of which she was found guilty.[23]

Napier was the victim of witchcraft accusation in a more familiar way: when Sampson was examined by judges, she accused, amongst others, her client of partaking in witchcraft. Certainly, out of concern for the health of her children, Napier might well have consulted Sampson, who certainly did have wealthy, and even aristocratic, clients. Napier, as is no doubt familiar to us by now, was accused of using magic to kill her husband and her rivals to secure favour and gain political power.

Neither woman arrived at court unprepared – Napier seems to have had a team of five lawyers, MacCalzean at least two – and the initial list of challenges to Napier's accusations lasted until two in the morning. One of MacCalzean's lawyers had even been King's Advocate two years earlier. Unfortunately, neither woman succeeded: they had fallen foul of contemporary readiness to believe that women were weak, ambitious and porous to sin. Natural victims for the Devil.

For Shakespeare's play, Macbeth's dealings with the witches represent the final disempowerment of Bothwell. He has enslaved himself to the slaves of Satan, and hitched his wagon to an empty throne. He is more than just doomed, he is cuckolded on the ultimate level by women who have given themselves to Satan. For King James, who celebrated his triumph over the Earl of Gowrie and the Ruthven Raiders for most of his life – and turned the failed Catholic plot against his life into a national holiday that still exists – the sight of Macbeth as a stand in for Bothwell, defeated by the witches' prophesy, would be fairly satisfying.

Selected References
[1] D M Palliser, *The Age of Elizabeth: England Under the Late Tudors 1547-1603*, Routledge,2013, loc. 3426
[2] Raphael Holinshed & Richard Horsley, *Holinshed's Chronicles of England, Scotland and Ireland*, 1577, Vol. 1, p. 94, accessed via The Holinshed Project:
http://english.nsms.ox.ac.uk/holinshed/texts.php?text1=1577_0068

[3] Keith Wrightson, *Early Necessities: Economic Lives in Early Modern Britain 1470-1750*, Yale University Press, 2002, p. 217

[4] Robert Wheaton, "Family and Kinship in Western Europe: The Problem of the Joint Family Household", *The Journal of Interdisciplinary History*, Vol. 5, No. 4, The History of the Family, II (Spring 1975), pp. 601–628; Edward Beaver, "Witchcraft, Female Aggression, and Power in the Early Modern Community", Helen Parish (ed), *Superstition and Magic in Early Modern Europe: A Reader*, Kindle Edition, Bloomsbury Academic, 2015, n. pag; Brian P Levack, *The Witch-Hunt in Early Modern Europe*, Third Edition, Routledge, 2006; Robin Briggs, *Witches and Neighbours: The Social and Cultural Context of European Witchcraft*, Second Edition, Kindle Edition, Blackwell, 2002

[5] Scott, pp. 5–6

[6] Sir James Melville, *Memoires of His Own Life by Sir James Melville of Halhill, 1549-1593, From the Original Manuscript*, The Bannatyne Club, 1827, p. 370

[7] Melville, p. 371

[8] Robert Pitcairn, *Ancient Criminal Trials in Scotland*, Vol. 1, Part 3, The Bannatyne Club, 1833, pp. 192–201

[9] Pitcairn, pp. 201–204; P G Maxwell-Stuart, *Satan's Conspiracy: Magic and Witchcraft in Sixteenth-Century Scotland*, Tuckwell Press, 2001

[10] Letter from John Chamberlain to Dudley Carleton, TNA SP 14/1/21

[11] William Camden, William Camden, Diary 1603–1623, Hypertext Edition, The Philological Museum, 2002, n. pag

[12] Normand & Roberts, p. 139

[13] Normand & Roberts, p. 138

[14] Normand & Roberts, p. 159

[15] Normand & Roberts, p. 160

[16] Normand & Roberts, pp. 163–167

[17] Normand & Roberts, pp. 171–173

[18] Normand & Roberts, pp. 309–353; John Newton (ed) & Jo Bath (ed), *Witchcraft and the Act of 1604*, Brill, 2008; James Shapiro, *1606 William Shakespeare and the Year of Lear*, Faber and Faber, 2015; James Sharpe, *The Bewitching of Anne Gunter: A Horrible and True Story of Football, Witchcraft, Murder, and the King of England*, Profile Books, 1999; Marion Gibson (ed), *Witchcraft and Society in England and America, 1550-1750*, Cornell University Press, 2003

[19] Jennifer Kolpacoff Deane, *A History of Medieval Heresy and Inquisition*, Rowman & Littlefield Publishers, Kindle Edition, 2011, loc. 4113; Also, Michel David Bailey, "The Feminization of Magic and the Emerging Idea of the Female Witch in the Late Middle Ages", *Essays in Medieval Studies*, Vol. 19, 2002, pp. 120–134

[20] Henry Goodcoal, "The Wonderfull Discoverie of Elizabeth Sawyer, a Witch", 1621, in Gibson, pp. 308–310

[21] P G Maxwell-Stuart, *Witch Beliefs and Witch Trials in the Middle Ages*, Continuum, Kindle Edition, 2011, p. 47

[22] "North Berwick witches (act. 1590–1592)," L. A. Yeoman in *Oxford Dictionary of National Biography*, Online Edition, ed. Lawrence Goldman, OUP
http://www.oxforddnb.com.ezproxy.londonlibrary.co.uk/view/article/69951

[23] Normand & Roberts, p. 291

Fairies

FAIRY:
Over hill, over dale,
Thorough bush, thorough brier,
Over park, over pale,
Thorough flood, thorough fire,
I do wander everywhere,
Swifter than the moon's sphere;
And I serve the fairy queen,
To dew her orbs upon the green.
The cowslips tall her pensioners be:
In their gold coats spots you see;
Those be rubies, fairy favours,
In those freckles live their savours:
I must go seek some dewdrops here
And hang a pearl in every cowslip's ear.
-- Act 2, Scene 1, A Midsummer Night's Dream, William
Shakespeare, (1595–6)

Whether in the antics of Oberon and Puck in *A Midsummer Night's Dream*, or in the retribution that the citizens of Windsor take against Sir John Falstaff in *The Merry Wives of Windsor*, Londoners – or, in fact, any citizen of the British Isles in the 16th and 17th century – would have been familiar with the idea of elves and fairies.

Certainly, not everyone believed in them. In the trial of Walter Ronalds, of Dyce near Aberdeen in 1601, the unfortunate defendant confessed to having been visited twice a year by an invisible spirit who would come and call out to him. For a while, Ronalds had not had any significant traffic with it, but in 1600 it sat next to his bed and appeared as a small, white-bearded man with white linen shift, who told him to go to a certain Welshman's house nearby, where he would be able to dig for vessels of gold and silver.

Unfortunately, for Ronalds, he was both a man of action and a man of tenacity: not only did he follow through on the spirit's suggestion, but after leaving empty handed he enlisted friends and family to search. Presumably turning the unfortunate Welshman's property into a ploughed field.

Fortunately for Ronalds – unlike another man visited by fairies, about whom we shall hear later – he was supported by his minister, William Nelson, who held that Ronalds was a good Christian and pledged to help him rehabilitate.

Some citizens of Shakespeare's era, however, were open to the idea that fairies lived around them. The Swiss theologian Ludwig Lavater, whose book *Of Ghosts and Spirits Walking by Night* was translated into English in 1572, wrote of the contemporary attitude to fairies:

"...hearing these things, I imagine, I knowe not howe, that there be certayne elves or fairies of the earth, and tell many strange and marvellous tales of them... even in these our days, in many places in the north parts, there are certayne monsters or spirites, which taking on them some shape or figure, vse (chiefly in the night season) to daunce after the sounds of all sorts of instruments of musicke: whome the inhabitants call companions of the daunces of fairies or elves..."[1]

From the Medieval era, chroniclers had recorded stories of the intimacy that our world had with that of the fairy realm. Gervaise of Tilbury, writing in 12th century Essex, recorded a story of a phenomenon in Catalonia, where knights would appear in the distance, battling fiercely, but vanish once a curious observer came close. More locally, he wrote of a rise in Wandlebury with a round earthwork, where a knight could battle a fairy if only he would come alone in the dead of night and call, "Let a knight come against a knight."

Geraldus Cambrensis, whose travel works give us tales of werewolfism and demonic possession, wrote of a tale he was told by a priest named Elidorus. While a boy in what is now Swansea, the young Elidorus had met with pixie-like fairies, not unlike the ones described in the above passage from *Midsummer* – small but well proportioned and riding specially adapted greyhounds in place of horses.

According to Elidorus the fairies were broadly Christian, living in a realm reached via subterranean passages, with a murky, cloudy sky that showed no moon or stars. Rather than being underground though, the fairy realm was a place on Earth: the antipode to the Christian kingdoms of Europe, where the fairies lived in a very much human society, except that they consumed only milk and saffron.

Even well after Shakespeare's lifetime, writers were recording belief in the fairies. Richard Bovert, in his 1684 book *Pandaemonium, or, the Devil's Cloyster*, describes a Somerset experience of fairies:

"…fairies or spirits, so called by the country people, which shewed themselves in great companies divers times; at sometimes they would seem to dance, at other times to keep a great fair or market…

"They are liked to appear nearest one side of a hill named Black-down between parishes of Pittminster and Chestonford, near Taunton... those that have had occasion to travel that way, have frequently seen them there appearing like men and women of a nature generally near the smaller size of men..."

Bovert relates the story of a neighbour coming home from a trip and finding what looked like a country fair:

"At length it came into his mind what he had heard of fairies on this side of the hill... he resolved to ride amongst them, and see what they were... though he saw them perfectly all along as he came, yet when he was upon the place... he could discern nothing at all, only seem to be crowded, and thrust, as when one passes through a throng of people: the rest became invisible... "He found himself in pain and so hastened home; where being arrived, a lameness seized him all on one side, which continued on him so long as he lived..."[2]

On the natural habitat of the fairies, the French scholar Pierre le Loyer, whose book *A Treatise of Specters or Straunge Sights, Visions or Apparitions* was translated in 1605 by Zachary Jones, writes on the natural habitat of fairies (who, as we shall examine later, he conflates with various classical spirits such as nymphs):

"...it hath beene continually held, and commonly thought, that the Spirits, and Nymphes, or Fayries haue loued ruinous places: and that for this cause the olde ruines of great, proud, & admirable buildings decayed haue been said to be the houses & dwelling places, or the workes of Nymphes? Surely as touching their inhabiting in ruinous places; Esay witnesseth it, where he sayeth, 'That the Syrens of Nymphes shall possesse their houses,

and their retrait & abiding.' The swellings of the
Nymphes described in Homer, and Virgil, are
sufficiently well knowne: that they were in dennes or
caues, farr remoued and concealed from the sight &
company of men: builded & wrought by themselves in
the natural rocks & hard stone. And Homer for his part
hath so well and perfectly described the Cauve of Ithaca,
where these Fayries did abide… besides the Temples of
the Nymphes… were always situated without the Citties
and Townes, in solitarie places, and farre remoued from
any dwellings…"[3]

Nor was the idea of fairies loving isolated places a
preserve of the elite. In the 1616 case of Elspeth Reoch,
the Cunning Woman Elspeth describes meeting her
fairies for the first time on a journey through the island
countryside:

"That she upon ane day being out of the loch in the
country and returning and being at the Loch syd awaiting
quhen the boat should fetch hir in. That their cum tua
men to her…"[4]

Another Scot, Andro Mann, described a scene
reminiscent of Bottom's experience in Titania's bower:

"Thow grantes the elphis will make the appear to be in a
fair chamber and yit, thow will find thy self in a moss
on the morne; and that they will appear to have candlis
and licht, and swordis, quilk wilbe nothing else bot dead
grass and strayes…"[5]

Likewise, in a passage reproduced from Jacob Boehme's
1623 book *Mysterium Magnum*, John Webster describes
a Cunning Man who claimed to have been given his
magical white powder by the fairies after knocking on

the side of a fairy hill – probably a barrow or other earthwork like the ones believed to be haunted by the then-forgotten Medieval revenant:

"What this man did was with a white powder which he said he received from the fairies, and that going to a hill he knocked three times, and the hill opened, and he had acces to, and converse with a visible peoples and offered, that if any gentleman present would either go himself in person, or send his servant, he could conduct them thither and shew them the place and person from where he had his skill…"[6]

Even Mary Parish, the scryer, wife and magical teacher of late 17th century nobleman Goodwin Wharton, met her fairies in an isolated location. Despite being an urban citizen, Wharton met her fairies on the third heath of Hounslowe, near a thatched manor that Charles II was using as a hunting lodge.

And so, whether to the common citizens who would have been watching *A Midsummer Night's Dream* from the yard of an amphitheatre, or if they were a later audience of the well to do – watching at one of the gilded indoor playhouses – the idea of fairies dwelling in the woods and ruins around Athens – even Shakespeare's fairly anglicised version – would have been both comfortable and fairly familiar: for the London labourer, it would have been resonant of the folk traditions of his daily life.

The Colours of Fairies

MISTRESS PAGE:
That likewise we have thought upon, and thus:
Nan Page my daughter and my little son
And three or four more of their growth we'll dress
Like urchins, ouphes and fairies, green and white...
-- Act 4, Scene 4, The Merry Wives of Windsor, William
Shakespeare, (1602)

Returning once more to Richard Bovert's 1684 account of fairy belief in Somerset, he describes very particularly the clothing of the fairies:

"their habits used to be of red, blew or green, according to the old way of country garb, with high crown'd hats..."

A more poetic description, not affecting any relation to reality, we see in the 1635 poem *A description of the king and queene of the fayries, their habit, fayre, their abode, pompe and state*. In it we see a very familiar colour palette, along with a similiarly romanticised description of their clothing to that of the fairies in Shakespeare's *A Midsummer Night's Dream*:

"First, a cobweb shirt, more
Thin than ever spider once
Could spin.
Chang'd to the whiteness
Of thy snow..."

Later, after some descriptions of waistcoats made from such substances as insects' wings and eunuch stubble, the author completes the green and white palette described in *A Midsummer Night's Dream*:

"The outside of his doublet was made of the four leaved, truye love'd grasse…"[7]

Again, James Hart's 1633 dietary text, *Klinike, or The Diet of the Diseased*, covers the belief in fairies, and more particularly categorises them in terms of colour:

"The white divells, the fairies, or rather (or as they say they were ordinarily to be seene) the green divells were want to pinch maids in the night time, if all were not cleane in the house."[8]

This patterning of white and green can also be seen in the Scottish trials. Elspeth Reoch's fairies are first described as, "tua men… one clad in black and the uther with ane grein tartane plaid about him…" In 1629 the confession of Janet Rendell describes meeting a man, "…above the hill of Rendell… clad in quhyte cloathis with one quhute head and ane grey beard."[9]

Even before these cases, the 1588 trial of Alesoun Piersoun describes a man in familiar clothing, appearing in the lonely and isolated setting of Grangemuir, which is now a woodland park on the opposite side of the Firth of Forth to North Berwick:

"that scho being in Grange-mure, with the folkis that past to the Mure, scho lay doun seik alane; and their come ane man to hir, cled in grene clathis…"[10]

This is very similar to a case that occurred fewer than ten years after the writing of *A Midsummer Night's Dream*, in 1607 in the village of Rye. As we have mentioned, Susanna Swapper was the scryer to local magician and possible chemical physician Anna Taylor – herself the daughter of a Cunning Woman. Anna and Susanna's relationship is one of ever shifting power dynamics, and offers a possible glimpse at a possible fairy faith that has been lost in records of English trials (and which we will examine later in this chapter). Swapper's first vision of the creatures she would later realise were fairies, might remind us very much of Alesoun Piersoun's experience. While sick in bed with a fever, she was visited by the fairies:

"about midelent last past she being in the chamber where she did lye with her husband in bed in the night tyme about the howers of twelve and one of the clock there appeared to her fower spirits in leiknes of two men and two women, the one of them being the tallest of the men was clothed in a whit surplice downe to the grounde being a younge man in countenance to her … without any heare on his face, the other man was a short thike man clothed all in whit with a satten dubblett and breeches … and a longe gray bearde, and one of the women was clothed with a greene petticoat and a white waistcoat with a Rayle about her neck and a whit kerchefe upon her head and a younge woman to her Judgement, the other was a young woman likenise clothed all in white, and so they continued two or three nighte together appearing unto her."[11]

Fairies – Between Good and Evil?

OBERON:
But we are spirits of another sort.
I with the Morning's love have oft made sport
And, like a forester, the groves may tread
Even till the easter gate, all fiery red,
Opening on Neptune with fair blessed beams,
Turns into yellow gold his salt green streams.
But, notwithstanding, haste, make no delay.
We may effect this business yet ere day.
-- Act 3, Scene 2, A Midsummer Night's Dream, William
Shakespeare, (1595–6)

Even at the level of elite theologians, fairies failed to find a true place in the cosmology of Christian Europe. Medieval romances had tried to fit them in as a neutral party in the war between heaven and hell – either conflating fairies with a faction of neutral angels or, as we see in *The South English Legendary*:

"There were others who, because their thoughts strayed somewhat
(even though they were more inclined to God, they barely held
themselves back) also departed from heaven, and they are above the
others, raised up below the heavens, and recognize God's will; and
so they must be punished somewhat until the end of the world, but
They shall return again to heaven at Doomsday."[12]

Other romances, like *Esclarmonde*, show a difference between neutral angels and fairies. When Huon races back to the deathbed of his fairy mentor Oberon, Huon meets a group of monks who are themselves neutral fairies, and certainly different to Oberon himself. In the Middle English version, the translator was careful to differentiate the neutral angels from either human or fairy, stating:

"[we] be conuerant amonge the people, & as well as they of the fayery… we be tho that hathe the conduct of al the fayery of the world…"

This middle ground, however, seems neither to have been accepted nor occupied by everyone. In the Scottish romance *Thomas of Erceldoune*, the fairies are put very firmly in their place. They may not be demons, but they are certainly a client nation of hell:

"Bot langere here thou may moghte duelle,
The skylle I sall the telle whare for:
To Morne, of hell the foulle fende
Amange this folke will feche his fee;
And thou art mekill mane and hende,–
I trowe full wele he wole chese the."
It is worth noting that in this version of the romance, the path to fairyland is one of five ways that Thomas may choose: to earthly paradise, to heaven, purgatory, or hell, and finally fairyland. Medieval chroniclers such as Walter Map and Gervase of Tilbury were eager to explain fairies away as a misapprehension of the past, lumped in with various evil and untoward spirits of the Classical era. In his *De Nugis Curialium*, Map describes the old world's misunderstanding of the nature of spirits, having one such spirit say:

"In old times the deluded people called us demi-gods or demi-goddesses, giving us names distinctive of sex, agreeable to the shape of the body or to the appearance we put on: and from the places we welt in or the functions allowed to us we are called hill-men, wood-men, Dryades, Oreads, fauns, satyrs, naiads, and our rulers (are christened by the people) Ceres, Baccus, Pan, Priapus, and Pales."[13]

In the Latin of the passages where Gervase discusses fairies and fairy motifs, he uses the terms Lamia, Lar, Larva, Strie and Masca in a barely defined way, agreeing with Augustine that a good spirit became a Lar, while an evil one became a Larva. We can see that this linguistic confusion was still very much the case in the 1649 primer *An Easie Entrance to the Latine Tongue*, by Charles Hoole. Here we see a mingling of positive and negative Latin baggage in the categorisation of supernatural beings and fairies:

"A damned spirit: spiritus infernalis
A divil: deamon, onis, m
The Divil: Diabolis, li, m
Satan: Satanus, ae. M
A fiend: furia, ae. F
Dead men's ghosts: Manes, ium
Walking spirits: Umbrae, arum
Spirits who walk at night amongst graves: Occursacula noctium, formidamina bustrorum
A sprite: Spectrum, tri. N
An ugly spirit: Mostellum, li.
A bug-bear: Terriculum, li
Fray-buggards: Moniae, arum
Fairies: lemuires, um, M
A fairy queen: Lamia, ae, F
An elf: Larva, ae, F
Fairies of the wood: Fauni, out
Fairies of the oakes: dryads
Fairies of the springs: nymphaea, arum, F

Fairies of the streams: Naiades
Fairies of the hills: Oreades
Fairies of the hous: Lares, ium"[14]

The list goes on, providing a fairly comprehensive
primer of supernatural terms for 17th century Latinists.
We can see this conceptual muddling at work even
earlier in Robert Burton's 1621 *Anatomy of Melancholy*,
where he characterises fairies as elemental beings – not
just Niaides or nymphs, but as elemental demons:

"Water divils, are those as Niades, or water nymphes,
which have been heretofore been conversant about
waters and rivers… some call them fairies and say that
Habundia is their queen, these cause inundations, many
times shipwrecks…

"Hotherus, a king of Sweden, that having lost his
company, as he was hunting one day, mette with these
water nymphs or fayries, and was feasted by them…"
On the more earth-based fairies, Burton also has a place:

"Terrestrial Divells, are those Genii, faunes, satyrs,
wood-nymphs, foliots, fairies, Robin Goodfellows…
which as they are most convwesant with men, so they do
them most harme…"
Finally he points out that some place fairies in a camp
with other earth spirits who have become renovated into
demonhood:

"Some put our fairies into their rank (with Dagon, Beli,
Astarte, Baal and other earth Gods), which have in
former times been adored with much superstition, with
sweeping their houses, with setting a pail of cleane
water, good victuals, and the like, and then they should

not be pinched, find money in their shooes, and be fortunate in their enterprises…"

"These are they that dance on heaths, as Lavatar thinks, and Olean Magnus, and are sometimes seene by old women and children… a bigger kind there is, called with us Hobgoblins, and Robin Goodfellows, that would in those superstitious times, grinde corne for a messe of milke, cut woode, or do any manner of drudgery work."[15]

However, there were still those who felt that fairies weren't all bad. In 1624 Thomas Jackson wrote his book *A treatise containing the original of unbeliefe, misbeliefe, or misperswasions concerning the veritie, unity and attributes of Deity*. Here he writes on various forms of mysticism, including the Neoplatonist belief in the magical properties of stones, but also on the popular belief in fairies. While Jackson's belief is clear, it is also clear that there were those who refused to accept that fairies were all bad:

"Thus are fayries, freom difference of events ascribed to them, divided into good and bad, when as it is but one and the same malignant fiend…"

He goes on to tell of a man who performed a magical experiment involving what he refers to as 'the falling of the fair seed', and when asking the magician what he thought would become of his disjecta, he was told:

"Why (quoth he)… doe you thinke that the devil hath ought to doe with that good seed? No; it is in the keeping of the king of fayries, and I know he will doe me no harme."[16]

Likewise, recognising, but ultimately rejecting this liminality, in 1691, the Puritan minister Richard Baxter wrote on the subject of fairies, with surprising nuance for a man of self-espoused Presbyterian and Nonconformist beliefs:

"Yea, we are not fully certane whether these aerial regions have not a third sort of wights, that are neither angels (good or fallen) nor souls of men, but such as have been placed as fishes in the sea, and men on earth: and whether these called fairies and goblins are not such…"[17]

Baxter went on to reject fairies as being in any way neutral, and to link them with a possession in Utrecht in 1625, where a woman suffered convulsions and where one child changed shape upon being exorcised. The Reverend Richard Greenham, similarly, had stated that his parishioners:

"…distinguished between [fairies] and other spirits, as commonly men distinguish between good witches and bad witches."[18]

Certainly the fairies were famed for causing illness. Earlier we read of our Somerset man who suffered what we would diagnose as a stroke after tangling with the fairies. Similarly, our Scottish fairy witch Elspeth Reoch suffered a similar symptom after finally submitting to her fairy mentor's amorous attentions:

"And upoun the third nycht that he com to hir she being asleep and laid his hand upon hir breist and walkint her. And thairefter semeit to ly with her. And upoun the morrow she had no power of hir tongue nor could nocht speik quhairthrow her brother dam hir with ane [bridle

for a horse] quhill she bled because she wald nocht speik
and pat one bow string abour hir head to gar her speik.
And tharafter tuik her three severall tymes sondayis to
the kirk and prayit for hir. Fra quhilik tyme she still
continewit dumb…"[19]

Nor was the phenomenon of stroke-like illnesses being
ascribed to the fairies unique to Elspeth or her home in
the Orkneys. In the trial of Jonet Morisone, of Bute, in
1662, Jonet confessed to being asked to heal a girl struck
sick in a very familiar way:

"being questioned anet her heiling of Mcfersone in
Keretoule his dochter who lay sick of a very unnaurall
disease without power of hand or foot both speichles and
kenured. She answered the disease quhilk ailed her was
blasting with the faryes and that she healed her with
herbes."
The deposition goes on to tell that she confessed to
healing two more people who had been struck a similar
way:

"…being questioned about her heileing of Alester
Bannatyne who was sick of the lyk disease answred that
he was blases with the fairyes and also that she heiled
him thereof with herbs and being questioned anent her
heileing of Patrick Glas dochter Barbra Glas answred
that she was blasted with the faryes also."[20]

Back in England, and much earlier, William Bullein, in
his 1579 book *Bullein's Bullwark of Defense*, wrote of a
Cunning Woman curing illness caused by the fairies in
Suffolk:

"A false witch, called Emmeline, in a town of Suffolk,
called Percham, which with a payre of Ebene beades and

certain charms, had no small resort of foolish woman, when their children were sick. To thys same wytch they resorted, to have the fairie charmed, and the spyrite coniured away: thoruhg the prayers of the Ebene beades…"[21]

In 1593 George Gifford's book *A Dialogue Concerning Witches* describes a similar cure for sickness:

"here lieth the deep subtiltie of Satan, how should the people be seduced to follow him, if he should not use great cunning to cover matters, as if devils were driven out, harmes cured that are done by them, even through the name and mightie power of God. Herein lieth a more foule abomination, and that is the abusing and horribly prophaning of the most blessed name of God, and the holy scriptures unto witcheries, charmes, coniurations, and unto devilish artes. Such an one is haunted with a fayrie, or a spirit: he must learn a charme compounded of some strange speaches, and the names of God intermingled, or weave some parte of S. John's Gospel of suchlilke…"[22]

Magicians had a similar trouble deciding where to put fairies. In V.b. 26, much of whose material is reproduced in Sloane MS 3851 – *The Grimoire of Arthur Gauntlet* – shows a difference of opinion throughout. The 'Names of the Seven Sisters of Fairies' are jotted down in the middle of an extended ritual to get the upper hand over thieves.

Later, 'Oberyon' and 'Mycob' are listed as very much demonic. While Oberyon is described fairly painstakingly as, "king of the fairies", nevertheless he appears in the same list as Lucifer. Mycob, the queen of the fairies, is once more described as being pleasant and gentle, but no mistake can be made that she is of the same cloth as her husband:

"Mycob is queen of the fairies, and is of the same office that Oberyon is of. She appeareth in green with a crown on her head, and is very meek and gentle. She showeth the nature of herbs, stone and trees. She showeth the use of medicine and the truth…"[23]

In the later leaves of the book, the 'figure' and seals of Oberyon are included in a section containing the clearly demonic 'Satan'. Although the various drawings of the demons seem to have been inspired by various depictions from the book *Cetaine Secrete Wonders of Nature* by Boaistuau and Fenton in 1569, with a circle and an elaborate set of conjurations that are, functionally, identical to the various procedures for summoning Baron or any other spirit.

For the 16th and 17th century magician, this mixture of caution and piety was critical. The euphemism 'spirit' appears much more in the workbooks of magicians than the more nuanced definitions of spirits that can be seen in books attributed to Solomon, such as the *Lemegaton* and *Clavicle of Solomon*. Demons are listed as 'spirits' next to planetary intelligences and kings of fairy. Yet the piety of the Renaissance ritual magician puts God above all of them: they are threatened, cajoled and pushed from pillar to post by the various names of God and tales of his great deeds.

Fairies and Mortals – Magic and Romance

For ritual magicians, and ordinary citizens, fairies could also be in cahoots with another part of the mystical world: witches. When the witchcraft believer Vicar of St. Brides, Henry Holland, wrote his reply to Reginald Scott's *The Discoverie of Witches*, he put women accused of practising witchcraft into very interesting company:

"…the witches are sometimes called Thessalae, Sagae, Wise Women, Magae, Persian Witches, Lamiae, Ladies of Fayrie, Striges, Hegges, and yet a witch is but a wicked man or woman that worked with the devil."[24]

The Grimoire of Arthur Gauntlet certainly classes fairies as a way that witches can vex a sorcerer's clients. Gauntlet wrote two separate spells for the curing of injuries and sickness inflicted by witches, both of which mention fairies, firstly:

"Call them I say into this Glass They being appeared say as followerth If there be but one witch and one spirit.

"O thou cursed and damned witch And thou Spirit of witchcraft and sorcerer's assistant to this hellish and cursed Creature by what name or title soever thou art called which dost hale pull terrify and torment the body carcass and limbs of AB of C in the county of D… I do bind you and charge you and command you and either of you upon pain and peril of your present and everlasting damnations That you nor neither of you neither that any other wicked witch Spirit or Fairies for you by you…"

"But if it be for a family and Cattle where there are more witches than one and many Spirit then work as followeth

and say.… O you cursed and Damned witches And you
Spirits of witchcraft And you fairie spirits Elves or
Pygmies Or by what other Style, name, Title or Addition
soever you are called… That you nor none of you neither
that any other wicked Spirit of Fairie…"[25]

The Scottish trials certainly showed witches and fairies
working together. Although Elspeth Reoch's fairy tutor
enacts a sexual liaison with her that crosses the line of
consent – begging the question of whether Elspeth was
playing out some real-life trauma – the method that he
uses to give her spirit sight is fairly similar to the
methods shown in V.b. 26 earlier:

"And the man with the plaid said to her she wes prettie.
And he wald lerne her to ken and sie any thing she wald
desire. The uther man said she wald nocht keep counsel
and foirbaid him. He answerit he wald [protect] hir. And
she being desirous to knaw said how could she ken that.
And he said tak an egg and rost it. And tak the sweit of it
thre Sonfayis and with [unwashed] handis wash her eyes
quhairby she sould sie and knaw any thing she
desyrit…"[26]

In fact, while Gauntlet seems to have been concerned
that witches and fairies were in cahoots to cause illness
and kill cattle, the Cunning Woman Bessie Dunlop, tried
in 1576, seems to have worked with her fairy familiar to
cure those afflicted by the fairies:

"…quehn sundrie persounes cam to hir to seik help for
their feist, their kow or yow, or for ane barne that was
tane away with ane evill blast of wind, or elf-grippt, sche
gait and speirit at Thom, Quhat mycht help thame?"[27]

The Cunning Women Janet Driver and Katherine Bigland, tried in 1615, certainly seemed to have a sexual and mutually beneficial relationship with the fairies. In addition to Katherine being able to ritually bathe and cleanse a man of demonic possession, Janet was designated:

"To be convict and giltie of the fostering of ane bairn in the hill of Westray to the fairy folk callit of hir our good neighbours… and having canal deal with hir. And having conversation with the fairy 26 yeiris bygare."[28]

The Cunning Man Andro Mann, tried in Aberdeen in 1597, seems to have both a fairly benevolent relationship with the queen of the fairies, and to have gained his medico-magical knowledge from her:

"The Devill, thy maister, com to thy motheris hous, in the liknes and schep of a woman, quhom thow callis the Quene of Elphen, and was delyverit of a bairne, as apperit to their, at quhil tyme thow being but a young boy, brought in water that devilische speirit, the Quene of Elphen, promesit to the, that thow suld knaw all thingis, and sulde help and cuir all sorts of seikness, except stand deid, and that theow suld be weill intenternit but wald seik thy meat or thow diet, as Thomas Rhymour did…[29]

"Thow condessis that thow can heal the falling seikness, barne, bed, and all sort of uther seikness…"

On the nature of his relationship with the Queen of Elphen – which might well simply have been a Presbyterian interrogator forcing Mann to agree to the most shocking arrangement he could imagine – Andro describes a fairly modern state of affairs:

"that the queen is very pleasant, and will be auld and young when she pleisis. Sche macks any [man] kyng quhom scho pleisis, and lyis with any scho pleisis."

Neither are the Scottish cases the only examples of fairies granting powers to their charges. In 1555, the Consistory Court of Wells tried local woman Joan Tyrrie, who blamed a period of blindness on the fairies. Like Andro Mann and Elspeth Reoch, she describes the fairies as helping her to divine who had bewitched whom and how to cure them:

"Joan Tyrrye personally appeared and confessed that the fayre Vayreis had told her… Simon Richardes had bewitched the wyffe and the Cattall of the foresaid David Morris. But she saethe sythens she was last examined she never sawe nor spake with the fayre vayreis and thinke she never shall because she hathe uttered theire secreates…"
Joan, like Andro and Elspeth, had been working with the fairies for some time – thirty years by her account – and had sought them both for knowledge and socialisation:

"by the helpe of the God and the fayre vayres with whom she hathe byn Accquaynted by the space of xxxtie yeres and more And hathe byn yn the companye of them manye and often tymes and hath byn merry yn theyre companye Daunceinge yn grene meadowes And worlde as glad to be yn the companye of them as anye gentelman or gentlewoman, for they have taught her such knowledg that she gettithe her Lyvynge by yt."[30]

While the possible fairy workings of Susanna Swapper and Anna Taylor of Rye – mentioned earlier – are the only examples of witchcraft defendants admitting fairy inspiration during Shakespeare's lifetime, it is certainly possible to show a continuity for the idea. As late as 1696, the London publisher Moses Pitt published a book regarding the Cunning Woman Ann Jeffries.

Here, Ann had been curing the sick and seemingly living without food for quite some time. If her own recollection is correct, she would have been 71 years old when Pitt's book was published, and had been seeing the fairies since she was 19. Pitt's account describes her as dancing with the fairies in her family's orchard, and as having lived without food for a year thanks to their charity in feeding her. With the exception of the resultant convulsive fit, the scene where she describes herself as meeting the fairies would suit as an excerpt from *A Midsummer Night's Dream*:

"In the year 1645 (she being 19 years old) she being one day knitting in an arbor in our garden, there came over the garden hedge to her six persons of a small stature, all clothed in green which were called fairies: upon which she was so frightened, that she fell into a kind of convulsion-fit…"[31]

In Pitt's account the fairies teach her how to cure the sick, and even show themselves to her sister, who offers a gift of a silver cup from them to her mother, which their mother tells her to send back.

For the modern reader, it is always tempting to interpret these accounts: Andro Mann could have been a lonely, unskilled man living with his mother. Elspeth Reoch could have invented her green man to work through a particularly traumatic assault. Ann Jeffries could have been either suffering from dementia, an overactive imagination, or schizophrenia. However, I feel very

strongly that we should neither label nor disempower
these people by putting ideas in their heads that might
not have been there, nor diagnosing them with conditions
that we cannot verify. Andro Mann is unavailable for
interview, and thus is protected from the categorisation
fetish of the modern world.

What is important for this book is this: a
Londoner living in Shakespeare's lifetime would likely
have known or known of someone claiming an intimate
relationship with the fairies. Whether by personal contact
or not, the stories of Bottom's intimacy with Titania and
the mother of the Indian changeling boy would have
been a part of their world.

Fairies and the Dead

PUCK:
My fairy lord, this must be done with haste,
For night's swift dragons cut the clouds full fast,
And yonder shines Aurora's harbinger,
At whose approach ghosts, wand'ring here and there
Troop home to churchyards. Damned spirits all
That in crossways and floods have burial,
Already to their wormy beds are gone.
For fear lest day should look their shames upon,
They willfully themselves exile from light,
And must for aye consort with black-browed night.

-- Act 3, Scene 3, A Midsummer Night's Dream, William Shakespeare, (1595–6)

That fairies' liminality – neither demon nor angel nor Homeric satyr – extends to the dead is hardly a surprise. What could be more ghostly than the idea of a will o'wisp, tempting travellers off the safe path in the marshes around London and getting them lost? That fairies had been associated with the dead can be seen in the 19th century work of folklorist Jessie Saxby, who recorded the story of Katherine or Kristin Fordyce, who had died in childbirth and her friends had failed to use the proper charms to protect her.

The result is that Katherine is portrayed as being 'Trowbound', a prisoner of the fairies after death who cannot leave because she has eaten fairy food. The unfortunate prisoner does seem to have some power though: she appears to her neighbour in dreams and offers various boons over their child, which is duly named after her, but is unable to escape fairy custody. In the last dream of the folktale, she is nursing a fairy child, pinned to a stone chair by an iron bar – hinting that her exposure to the fairies has given her some of their traditional weaknesses to iron.[32]

While this is a modern folktale, the experience of a member of Shakespeare's audiences might well have given them the same ideas. In the confession of Andro Mann, when questioned about his time in the Queen of Elphen's home he confessed that, "[he] kennis sindrie deid men in thair companie, and that the kyng that deit in Flowdown and Thomas Rhymour are there…"

Andro Mann's spirit, Christonday, was at least a member of the queen's household; Bessie Dunlop's fairy familiar – respectably clothed and holding a white wand much like Joan Tyrrie's first fairy encounter in Taunton market – was one of the dead men seen at her court. Joan's deposition to the court describes him as having died at the battle of Pinkie some years before the trial. Likewise, Alesoun Piersoun's 'familiar' was another dead man with ties to the fairies: a relative of hers named William Sympsoun who, like Bessie Dunlop's spirit, acted not just to teach her mystical knowledge, but to prevent the Queen of Elphen – with whom Alesoun admits to having a good relationship – from overpowering Alesoun and taking her away permanently. Even Elspeth Reoch's ghost/fairy mentor, John Stewart, operates in a similar way, saying that he would protect her.

This permeable relationship between fairies and the dead can also been seen in the overlap between fairies and the phenomenon that modern readers would call a poltergeist. In Burton's 1621 work, he writes not just of elemental fairies and hobgoblins, but of fairies who haunt:

"Another kinde of those there are, wich frequent folorne house… they will make strange noyses in the night, sling stones, rattle chaines, shave men, sling downe platters, stooles, chests, sometime appeare in the likeness of hares, crowes, frogges, dogges, &c…"[33]

Thomas Johnson's translation of the 16th century French surgeon Ambrose Paré's works, while sceptical, describe a very similar vein of belief, and much the same culprit:

"They houle on the night, they murmure & rattle… they move benches, tables, counters, props, cupboards, children in cradles, play at tables and chesse, turn over books, tell money, walk up and down rooms, and are heard to laugh, to open windows and dores, cast sounding vessels, use brasse and the like, upon the ground, break store pots and glasses, and make other noises. Yet none of these things appear to us when we arise in the morning, neither find we any thing out of its place or broken. They are called diverse names; as Devilles, evil spirits, Incubi, Succubi, Hobgoblins, Fairies, Robin Goodfellowes, evill Angells, Sathan, Lucifer…"[34]

Both in writing in 1635, Thomas Heywood and William James describe a fairy tradition wherein fairies appear as a as a sort of house-disturbing 'noisy spirit' that haunts lonely places. For James it is a superstitious holdover from Catholicism:

"In the time of popery, the people were much deluded with the walking of spirits, they durst not go through a church-yard in the night for fear of them. Sundry are afraid of fairies and of ill spirites that haunt their houses: no doubt but the evil angels are busy in all places."

While for Heywood fairies are definitely Satanic, but his opinion of their existence is more certain:

"Robin Goodfellows, some call them fairies
In solitary rooms these uproarers keep
and beat at dores to wake men from their sleepes
seeming to force locks, be they ne're so strong
and keeping Christmass gambols all night long
Potts, glasses, trenchers, dishes, pannes and kettles
they will make dance about shelves and settles
as if the kitchen tost and cast
yet in the morning nothing found misplac't."[35]

That fairies occupy a hinterland between so many territories is hard to lay at the door of any one group. The Latin word games of the Medieval and Early Modern thinkers muddied the waters between fairies and larvae, and Titania and Lamia, but what of Joan Tyrrie whose first fairy held the same white wand as Bessie Dunlop's ghost mentor? What of the fairy hills that corresponded to the burial sites and earthworks where Medieval thinkers had also housed the revenants and the ancient undead? Would the 14th century Bylands manuscript, with its intelligent, articulate, shape changing ghosts have been a collection of literal fairy tales if it had been written 200 years later? Or in the South of England? Even Theseus, brave leader of Athens and relatively benevolent ruler over the human element of Shakespeare's characters, advises his subjects to retire, not only because they will arise late, but because they have slipped into the period where the world does not belong to them.

THESEUS:
The iron tongue of midnight hath told twelve:
Lovers, to bed; 'tis almost fairy time.
-- Act 5, Scene 1, A Midsummer Night's Dream, William Shakespeare, (1595–6)

Fraudulent Fairies

FALSTAFF:
And these are not fairies? I was three or four
times in the thought they were not fairies: and yet
the guiltiness of my mind, the sudden surprise of my
powers, drove the grossness of the foppery into a
received belief, in despite of the teeth of all
rhyme and reason, that they were fairies. See now
how wit may be made a Jack-a-Lent, when 'tis upon
ill employment!

-- Act 5, Scene 5, The Merry Wives of Windsor, William
Shakespeare, (1597)

Oddly, one of the strongest proofs that some citizens of
Shakespeare's era believed in fairies is that it was
possible to cheat them out of house and home by
offering them various forms of fairy favour. In *The
Merry Wives of Windsor*, Mistress Quickly and the
others play a trick on Falstaff, using lines very
reminiscent of Shakespeare's other fairy play, which
would have been performed for the first time in 1596, or
some time the year before.

Pierre le Loyer, translated by Zachary
Jones in 1605, wrote of schoolboy high jinks,
making citizens think their cemeteries were
haunted by will o'wisps by putting candles on
the backs of tortoises, and of Swiss revellers
frightening children while wearing masks
depicting fairies.[36]

In the same year marked as the earliest
audiences could have seen Shakespeare's *A
Midsummer Night's Dream*, 1595, a pamphlet
was published, depicting the crimes of Judith
Phelps, who had defrauded a wealthy widow by

pretending to have communication with the Queen of the Fairies. After drawing the woman in with the sorts of cold-reading tricks used to bamboozle old people to this day, Phelps persuaded the widow that her husband had hidden a considerable treasure in the house.

The solution proposed by Phelps was a ceremony: candlesticks were set around the house and Phelps said various prayers – likely not dissimilar to those in V.b. 26 or *The Grimoire of Arthur Gauntlet* – and directed the widow to wrap a purse containing £100 in a ball of woollen yarn. This, of course, was the aim of the con, and during the whole proceeding Phelps managed to substitute the purse for one filled with stones, and to escape by telling the widow that she needed to consult with a Cunning Man who was acquainted with the Queen of the Fairies.

It was returning from this consultation that saw Phelps caught: she came back to advise the widow of another, more elaborate, ritual involving gold coins, and was promptly arrested.

Another tale from the same pamphlet – and one that it is easily imaginable as giving Shakespeare inspiration for the tricking of the lustful Falstaff – is the actual bridling of a victim that gives Phelps' pamphlet its name.

This story, where Phelps is also reported as getting her just desserts, takes place in Hampshire, where Phelps was practising as a Cunning Woman. According to the pamphlet, one of her neighbours was "[a] wealthy churl… somewhat fantastical and given to believe every tale he heard…"

After a suitable performance of mystical knowing, Phelps persuaded the man and his wife that the tree in their garden was the site of buried treasure. This was not an unknown belief. In 1607 in Rye, Anna Taylor – of whom we have heard – was also convinced that a

tree in her garden was the site of buried
treasure. After Susanna had started having
visions of the fairies, Mrs Taylor had explained
their connection to valuables that she believed
were hidden in her garden:

"Mrs. Tayler setting by her did tell this examinate that
one Pywell which did dwell in the house where this
examinate now dwelleth was troubled in like sort, and
she caused him to dig before that tyme for money in her
garden and so he digged so farr until he came nere unto
it, and when he had digged neare unto it the said Pywell
being afraide he would needs call Mrs. Taylor which
accordingly he did, and then Mrs. Taylor cominge to the
place where he digged she said the futher they digged the
further the money was off, but she said she was heire to
the money and therefore it was gode will that she should
not enioy it, and then she bid Pywell digge further and
feare not for she was with childe and I hope in god
nothing will hurt us, but Pywell was feareful and his
culler vaded away and she thought in her conscience that
he died of it and after this speache Mrs. Tayler willed her
that yf the spiritte should appeare unto her againe in
reygarde they had digged already and could finde
nothing, that she shoulde ask them some more in any
other place, and that yf she did finde the money she
would geve unto this examinate one hundred poundes,
and that she and her children should never want whilest
she lived…"[37]

In the case of Mrs Taylor, neither Susanna nor Pywell
were likely the first to have dug for treasure in Mrs
Taylor's garden, or at least to have been asked to do so.
The tailor Phillip Williams (an easily impoverished
profession, tailors sometimes turned to having to
supplement their income) gave a statement that he had

been labouring in the Taylors' garden some time in 1605 when George Taylor had introduced a very strange topic of conversation:

"…this examinate did labour in his garden by the space of a weeke or thereaboutes, and being there at worke Mr Taylor did shewe unto this ex a place in the garden nere unto the somer howse and the said Mr Taylor did say unto him this ex the place that Pywell did dig in that garden for money. And that there was treasure hide there as he had heard and that if this ex had a stomacke to dig for and hee might… Mrs Taylor did speake unto this examinate div'se tymes to dig in the said place, assuring him that there was treasure hide there…."[38]

In the case of Judith Phelps' unfortunate victim, she managed to convince both the man and his wife that there was certainly treasure: after her mystical performance and a little cold reading, she persuaded them to dig under the tree, where they found some coins that Phelps herself had planted there a little while earlier.

With her victims hooked, she named a fee of £14 for the ceremony that would bring the 'Queen of the Fairies' to earthly appearance and grant them the treasure. Phelps demanded that the largest chamber in the house was decorated suitably for the ritual, which her marks complied with.

Finally, however, she introduced an element both strange and sadistic: she saddled the 'churl' himself – her victim – and rode him three times between the ritual chamber and his house, finally directing him and his wife to lie prostrate in front of the tree… while she went inside and stripped their home of valuables. Eventually, of course, the man and his wife realised what had happened to them – despite Phelps briefly

masquerading as the fairy queen on her way out
– and managed to have her arrested.

Another criminal partnership playing
on belief in the fairies were John and Alice
West, whose pamphlet debut came in 1613.
Their victim that year had been a Thomas More
of Hammersmith. After learning of his belief in
the existence of fairies, the Wests chose their
mark:
"[they claimed] to be familiarly acquainted with the king
and Queene of the fairies, who that had in their power
the command of inestimable treasure…"

The Wests persuaded the family's
maid to say that she had suffered a vision
showing her that the king and queen of the
fairies had appeared, "Saying that they had a
purpose to bestow great summes of gold upon
this man and woman…"

The con itself was more subtle than
Phelps: after swearing her clients to secrecy,
Alice and John charged them more and more
money for special equipment to summon the
fairies, including a full banquet and several
vessels that she promised the fairies would fill
with treasure.

Not that the Wests were any more
moral than Judith Phelps: on the Strand they
robbed a maid by making her sit naked with a
pot in her lap that they promised would be filled
with treasure – meanwhile they stole her clothes
and seven years' savings. They took livestock
from country folk, promising reward in the
services of fairy pages.

Similarly to Judith, Alice also
convinced a gentlewoman that she brought a
message from the queen of the fairies, and

tricked her out of a number of gold coins under the pretext of wrapping them specially in linen so that they would increase in number. Alice also persuaded a country widow that she was partly of fairy heritage herself – in order to part her from two jewelled rings that she stole after a ceremony that was supposed to be a sacrifice to the king of the fairies.

An additional attempt at fleecing this country widow was Alice's undoing. She was arrested when she returned to the house for another 'ceremony'. But by far the most violent act of the partnership belonged to her husband, who persuaded a goldsmith's apprentice that he had attracted the romantic attention of the queen of the fairies, and that if he brought various pieces of silver plate out to a close in St. Giles, she would turn them to gold. The young man did so, but not liking their chances against a young man instead of an old woman, Alice and John beat him with brickbats, leaving him injured and stealing his master's wares.[39]

It is possible to say that the various victims of Judith Phelps and the Wests were credulous – some commentators in their own time would have – but they prove that without doubt, for some members of Shakespeare's audience, the fairies and their monarchs would have been a fact of life rather than a fancy. Both of Shakespeare's 'fairy' plays came at the start of a dramatic spike in published concern about fairies – with the market seeing a pronounced spike in titles covering fairies from 1598 to 1610.

Final Thoughts

Shakespeare and his contemporaries were living in the time of Scott and Wier's sceptical work, in a time when a changing legal system was forcing both writers and citizens to think in a new way about the delineation between objective and subjective experience. However, none of the crimes perpetrated could have been performed without a firm, unshakable belief in the supernatural, and none of these people were mentally deficient: in order to be worth stealing from they had to be both shrewd in business and fairly good with their money. Their only weakness was in being a product of their time.

Selected References

[1] Ludwig Lavatar, *Of Ghosts and Spirits Walking by Night*, 1572, n. pag

[2] Richard Bovert, *Pandaemonium or, The Devil's Cloyster*, 1684, n. pag

[3] Pierre le Loyer & Zachary Jones (tr), *A Treatise of Spectres or Straunge Sights, Visions or Apprehensions*, 1605, p. 55

[4] G F Black & N W Thomas, *Examples of Printed Folklore Concerning the Orkney and Shetland Islands*, Country Folklore, Vol. 3, The Folklore Society, 1903, pp. 111–115

[5] John Stuart (ed), *The Miscelleny of the Spalding Club*, Vol. 1, 1841, pp. 119–125

[6] Jacob Boeheme, "Mysterium Magnum" in John Webster, *The Displaying of Supposed Witchcraft*, 1677, pp. 300–301

[7] R S, *A Description of the King and Queene of the Fayries, Their Habit, Fare, their Abode, Pompe and State*, 1635, n. pag

[8] James Hart of Northampton, *Klinike, or the Diet of the Diseased*, 1633

[9] Black & Thomas, pp. 103–108

[10] Pitcairn, p. 163

[11] TNA RYE 1/13/1

[12] Richard Frith Green, *Elf Queens and Holy Friars*, University of Pennsylvania Press, 2016, pp. 22–26

[13] Walter Map & M R James (tr), *De Nugis Curialium, or The Trifles of the Courtiers*, Clarendon Press, Revised Edition, 1994, p. 321

[14] Charles Hoole, *An Easie Entrance to the Latine Tongue*, 1649, n. pag

[15] Robert Burton, *The Anatomy of Melancholy What it is*, 1621, n. pag

[16] Thomas Jackson, *A Treatise Containing the Originall of Unbelief, Misbeliefe, or Misperswasions Concerning the Veritie, Unitie and Attributes of Deity*, 1624, n. pag

[17] Richard Baxter, *The Certainty of the Worlds of Spirits*, 1691, n. pag

[18] Reverend Richard Greenham, *The Works of the Reverend and Faithfull Servant of Jesus Christ M. Richard Greenham*, 1612, n. pag

[19] Black and Thomas, pp. 111–115

[20] J R N MacPhail, *The Highland Papers*, Vol. 3, Edinburgh University Press, 1920, pp. 23–24

[21] William Bullein, *Bullein's Bullwark of Defense*, 1579, n. pag

[22] George Gifford, *A Dialogue Concerning Witches and Witchcrafts in Which is Laid Open How Craftely the Divell Deciveth Not Only the Witches but Many Other and So Leadeth Them Awrie Into Many Great Errores*, 1593, n. pag

[23] Harms, Clark and Peterson, p. 207

[24] Henry Holland, *A Treatise Against Witchcraft: or a Dialogue Wherein the Greatest Doubts Concerning That Sinne, Are Briefly Answered*, 1590, n. pag

[25] Rankine, pp. 123–126

[26] Black & Thomas, pp. 111–115

[27] Pitcairn, p. 53

[28] Black & Thomas, pp. 72–74

[29] Stuart, pp. 119–125

[30] Somerset Heritage Centre deposition books D/D/ca 21 and D/D/ca 22

[31] Moses Pitt, *An Account of Anne Jeffries*, 1696

[32] Black & Thomas, pp. 23–24

[33] Robert Burton, *An Anatomy of Melancholy*, 1621, n. pag

[34] Ambrose Paré & Thomas Johnson, *The Works of That Famous Chiurgeon Ambrose Parey*, n. pag

[35] Thomas Heywood, *The Hierarchie of the Blessed Angels*, 1635, n. pag

[36] le Loyer & Jones, p. 181, p. 237

[37] TNA RYE 1/13/1

[38] TNA RYE 1/13/4

[39] Anon, *The Severall Notorious and Lewd Cousnages of John West and Alice West, Falsely called the King and Queen of the Fayries*, 1613, n. pag

Index

About the Author

Jon Kaneko-James is an Early Modern historian who works as a tour guide at Shakespeare's Globe. In the past he has worked in such salubrious jobs as dogsbody at a fetish club, bookseller, smalltime magazine typesetter, Tarot card reader, Soho cloakroom attendant, kitchen porter, not-particularly-good-farm-laborer and a waiter at a late-night steak house that nobody ever went to for the food.

His other books can be found on Amazon.

More of his historical writing can be found on www.jonkanekojames.com

Lightning Source UK Ltd.
Milton Keynes UK
UKHW04f2059031018
329934UK00001B/309/P

9 780995 778412